The Ninth Child

Book II – Biretta

By

George B. Van Antwerp

Van Antwerp and Beale Publishers

D0110388

Van Antwerp and Beale Publishers

2222 Lloyd Avenue, Royal Oak, Michigan 48073-3849
(248) 541-1788 — E-Mail: gvanantwerp1@comcast.net
International Standard Book Number 0-9727590-1-8
Printed in the United States
First Edition
Library of Congress Control Number
2003100497

Dedication

To my friends,
wherever I have worked
my fellow priests (the biretta boys) and
parishioners, religious women, Peace Corps
staff & Volunteers, Mount Carmel
Hospital staff, Shar House staff,
Southwest Counseling and Development,
Society of St. Vincent de Paul, Boniface
Human Services, migrant farm workers,
the Latinos, the people with problems and
their social workers,
those who feel forgotten and alone,
my wonderful brothers and sisters,
but mostly my wife and children
each of whom I love so much

George Van Antwerp

author

George Van Antwerp, M.Div., C.S.W.

George has helped people improve their lives for over 50 years. His skills in management, innovation, communication, public relations and fund development have been dedicated to non-profit charitable organizations.

Coming as the ninth child in a family of eleven children, George has been able to work with many wonderful and dedicated people in a variety of roles and settings. These include as a priest serving in churches and as a layman working in Peace Corps areas, rehabilitation programs, and hospital departments. He is an innovator and developed new approaches to teaching groups in English, Spanish and Portuguese. He started two credit unions in two places, formation programs in Brazil, used new approaches to migrant farm worker services and Catholic parish programming, unionized bill-passers on Detroit's Skid Row, began new programs (community mental health, Cursillo, Marriage Encounter, missions to Dominican Republic and Brazil), started the Prestige Club for Hospital retirees, and a Tuesday morning prayer group for priests, to name a few.

He has always been a good communicator. This is shown by his extensive public speaking experience, editor of many newsletters, he had several radio programs, taught high school classes for ten years, directed an effective Public Relations Department.

George received his college education at Sacred Heart Seminary in Detroit. He was awarded a Masters Degree in Divinity from St. John's Provincial Seminary. He did postgraduate studies at the University of Detroit, as well as in Mexico City, Puerto Rico and Brazil.

As a volunteer, he has been chairman of the Fr. Clement H. Kern Foundation, the Michigan League for Human Services, the Latino Cultural Pastoral Center, Detroit Citizens for Good Public Schools and Citizens for Residency of Detroit Police Officers. He also volunteers at the George Crockett Academy, the Knights of Columbus, the National Shrine of the Little Flower and Farm Worker Health Services.

Recent honors include awards from the *Latino Cultural Pastoral Center, the Society of St. Vincent de Paul, SHAR Foundation, Northwest Area Business Association* and the *Chamber of Commerce/Detroit Police Community Award.*

George was married in 1970 to Mary Lou (nee Beale). They have three children, George, Karon, and Michael.
The 2002 photo below shows George and Mary Lou holding their granddaughter, Keeley. In the rear (l to r) are Karon, Mike, Ami Field (Mike's fiancé), Kerri (George's wife) and George

prologue

… another word with you, the reader

This is Book II telling stories of my experiences for the second part of my life. I know you will enjoy some of the stories. I don't write these books as ego trips, but simply to share with you some stories and perhaps a glimpse of the values and hopes that my family, my friends and my faith have given to me.

In this book, I talk about my work as a priest in several settings. In Book III, I will tell stories about my "second incarnation" as a married man and father of three.

I love the Catholic priesthood, and wait for the day it will include women and married persons. I love the Catholic Church with all its many, many faults, both historically and presently. I also love married life, and my wonderful wife and children.

As I write, I smile at happy memories, and want to kick myself for being so naïve or dumb so often, and other times I have tears in my eyes, recalling the wonderful people I knew who were so good.

Thanks to my diligent proofreaders, my close friend, Roger Playwin, my sister, Dacia Van Antwerp, my brother, Dan Van Antwerp and my wonderful wife, Mary Lou.

Many people felt they were left out of my first book. They might be omitted in this one too. This doesn't mean I have forgotten them. I just can't put each of you in this book or I'll never finish it! I still love you!

These are my life experiences as the ninth child of Eugene Ignatius Van Antwerp and Mary Frances McDevitt – a life I really have enjoyed.

Special Note:
The Biretta:

The biretta is worn by Roman Catholic clergy for official occasions. It dates back to the Middle Ages when tonsured clergy wore a skullcap with a tuft on top to protect their bare heads. Ecclesiastical rank is indicated by the color of the tassel on top, even the color of the whole biretta. Cardinals wear red; bishops, purple; and diocesan clergy, black. Since Vatican Council II (1962-1965), clergy have dressed more like their parishioners, and birettas are now seldom worn. I haven't worn one since arriving at Most Holy Trinity Church in 1959.

The Ninth Child

Contents

11

priesthood

Ordination And The New Feeling – Was It Right?

The big day finally arrived! June 6th, 1953. I was to be ordained a Roman Catholic priest by **Edward Cardinal Mooney**, the Archbishop of Detroit in the Cathedral of the Most Blessed Sacrament on Woodward Avenue at Belmont in Detroit, Michigan, USA.

Days, months and years of preparation were now history. Four years of graduate study in moral and dogmatic theology, canon law, sacred scripture, church music, public speaking, biblical languages of Latin, Hebrew, and Greek, even classes on social justice and polite manners --- these were summed up in our final oral examinations covering our years of study. Previously, we had received the "minor orders" and then we were ordained on separate occasions as subdeacons, then as deacons. No more practicing Mass or absolution. Now it would be the real thing.

I don't remember much about that day. It went so fast. I do recall how nervous I was when I had to promise obedience to my bishop. I kept responding in English, "I promise" three times when I was supposed to say "Promito" (Latin is the official Church language). So as my folded hands were clasped by the hands of the Cardinal, **Monsignor Joe Breitenbeck**, the cardinal's master of ceremonies who later became Bishop of Grand Rapids, finally had to tell me "George, just say 'Promito'". He kidded me about that many times later.

Something else happened that day which is harder to explain. Becoming a priest changes your relationships with people. I guess it is the "awe" that so many Catholics have for their priests. All of a sudden, people treated me differently. Like I was suddenly holy, immediately wise and all-knowing. From that day forward, people would listen to my words of wisdom, kneel before me for my blessing (even my parents!!), give me the best seat at school plays, put me first in line for meals in church basements, even the police hesitated to give me traffic tickets. People, even very poor people, gave me gifts, stores gave me discounts, strangers told me their most intimate secrets, and, most humbling of all, they laughed at all my jokes (even when I knew they really weren't that funny!).

There is both a good and a bad side of this. The good is that, in my opinion, "respect" for people holding certain positions in society is a healthy thing. My Dad taught me to always respect the president of the United States, the governor, the mayor, judges and all public officials and all ministers of religion. This is because of the office they hold. You might not like or admire the person, but you should respect the office. He taught me this especially when we heard of people "booing" **President Truman** at Yankee Stadium shortly after he removed popular **General MacArthur** from his command in the Far East for disobeying an order. I learned soon that "respect" is healthy and good in society.

The unhealthy side is when citizens or, at least in this case, Catholics, refrain from properly criticizing the actions of those leaders out of "respect". All of us have a right, even a duty, to speak out for justice, to seek address of our grievances. This includes priests who should not sexually abuse children or even drive a car recklessly. Speak up!

I suppose that similar things happen to others – lawyers who are selected judges and medical students who become doctors, just to name a few. However, I never felt comfortable with the deferences nor the "freebies". I never felt smarter or holier since I knew so many others who were smarter and holier. I did accept the honors, though, knowing it wasn't anything personal, which is how most priests handle it. The honors were given because of the priesthood, which I still believe is something very special.

I also believe that this "special" priesthood will include married persons, male and female. It should. The times have changed!

Lauretta and Juge Came With All Eleven

My ordination day was enriched immensely when my sister, **Lauretta**, and her husband, **Julius Jaeger** (whom we call "Juge") were able to be in Detroit with all of their eleven children. Juge worked (until he retired in 1988) for Lockheed. He had been working for them in Burbank, California but was being transferred to their new plant near Atlanta, Georgia.

The timing was right. Juge arranged for his whole family to remain in Detroit for several days. They would stay for my ordination and first Mass. Two of their daughters (as well as four other nephews and nieces) made their First Communion at that Mass.

Except for my two sisters, **Dolores** and **Dacia**, who were in the convent and not allowed to come home, all of my other brothers and sisters were on hand for these special days.

My first Mass was celebrated at Gesu Parish in Detroit on June 7th, 1953. **Father Moore, S.J.**, the pastor, gave the sermon. My uncle, **Father Francis F. Van Antwerp**, then pastor of St. Ambrose Parish in Grosse Pointe, was the archdeacon. My brother, **Father Gene**, was deacon. My cousin, **Father John G. Van Antwerp**, then pastor of St. Edith Parish in

Livonia, was subdeacon. My cousins, **Father Thomas J. Van Antwerp** and **Fr. George Reno, S.J.** assisted. My seminarian cousin, **Tom McDevitt**, now a retired priest from the Lansing, Michigan diocese, also assisted. The 4th Degree Knights of Columbus and the members of the Alhambra Society were on hand. The church was packed. *(See the photo of religious in the family on page 57.)*

Even Conrad Hilton Showed Up

Dad took special pride in the Veteran's Memorial Building at the Detroit riverfront next to Cobo Hall. For decades, he had campaigned with many other veterans for the city to build it to honor its veterans. (I understand that it may soon be torn down!). I had wanted to have the breakfast and reception after my first Mass in our parish basement hall at Gesu, but they were finishing an auditorium/gym on top of it and construction work would not permit such an event. Naturally, the Veteran's Memorial was the only place Dad wanted to have it. So there it was held!

Well, you'd think the Pope had come. Over two hundred for breakfast (I know the count – Dad made me pay!) and over six hundred showed up for the Reception. Every politician in town, every labor leader, many businessmen, and, naturally, all of the **Van Antwerp and McDevitt relatives** showed up. Even **Conrad Hilton**, who was busy building hotels around the world, came to ask for my blessing. I still have the Guest Register with all of their names. No, I won't list them here. But you would recognize many of their names, I'm sure.

I only write about this day because it was so important in my life, to me, my parents and my family. I'm sure you have had days that you also remember as highlights in your life. Those days were very special to you but might not be to those outside your family.

A Few Stories About Adrian

My first parish assignment was by letter, stating that I was to report to St. Mary's Church in Adrian, Michigan, where I was to serve as the assistant pastor, under my cousin, **Father George H. Kerby**.

Now, I was a "Detroit" boy. City. Sure I had visited Mexico. I had traveled around the country with Dad when he served as Commander-in-Chief of the V.F.W. But, I ask you, what normal Detroit boy would have any idea where in the world a town called Adrian was? I got out a map. I looked for it. It wasn't around Pontiac. Not near Monroe. Not around Port Huron. I found it!! There it is, see, way over there!

Let me tell you a few stories about Adrian, a small, growing, friendly town that came to be my "first love".

Is This It? – Arriving in Adrian

 I felt like **Bing Crosby** in *"Going My Way!"* – presumptuous, so I never told anyone.

But here I was, on my way to my first assignment as a priest, in my brand new '53 Chevrolet (cost me $1,850!!). It was plain and black, as befitting a new, young priest. It didn't have 25 miles on it when I started on the road to Adrian, map in hand, since I still wasn't sure where it was. I had spoken with my new pastor, **Father Kerby**, on the phone for directions. He told me of a "short cut" (an illusion, of course – there is no such thing as a short cut to Adrian!). He told me that, if I turned left off of US-12 (Michigan Avenue) at the town of Clinton, and headed south past the potato farms to Tecumseh, there was a road east out of Tecumseh that would take me right to Adrian.

I followed his directions as best as I could. Even got to Tecumseh. Aha! I saw a road with a sign (arrow) that read "Adrian", which I followed to the end. At the end of that road (the paved part) there was an intersection with a blinker and a settlement. Just a blinker! Not even a red light! Geez. So this was Adrian! Where is downtown? I spotted a store advertising hunting and fishing gear, as well as boats.

Okay. So where's the church? Dumb me, right across the street was a large, wooden church, painted white, with a rectory alongside. I looked for a sign and saw none, but that's the way many Catholic churches were in those days. I drove into the gravel parking lot wondering if I should start carrying my things up to the door right away. I didn't own many "worldly goods", mostly books and my golf clubs – necessary tools of the active ministry. No, I decided. First go in, say hello to the pastor, then go back to the car for my things.

It has been said that when you frighten a rabbit, the poor little thing scampers off in a hurry. So do bank robbers when the alarm goes off. When I, as a brand new Roman Catholic priest, with breviary in hand

and wearing my new Sunday black suit and Roman collar, spotted the Baptist church sign on my way to the "rectory", I will bet that I beat the world record for scared rabbits and nervous bank robbers in retreating to my car, starting the motor and disappearing down the road!!

Adrian, Adrian, where art thou?

Jaw-urge, Let Me Tell You About Religion

Adrian was a Methodist town, it turned out. There were 26 churches of varying denominations, even a Catholic "motherhouse" of wonderful Dominican nuns, but the Methodists really controlled the town, I soon realized.

I remembered what **David Lucas** had explained to me while we walked on the sands of Myrtle Beach when we were twelve. He was my close friend every summer and was from Charlotte, North Carolina. I must have talked too "Catholic" for him. "Jaw-urge", he said, using the North Carolinian pronunciation of my given name. He always said it slowly when he was going to say something important to me. "Let me tell you about religion here in the South", he continued. "The Episcopalians, we are at the top, under us are the Presbyterians, then the Methodists, and at the bottom are the Baptists. And way under them are the Catholics".

I had been brought up in a Catholic enclave even with many friends of other faiths. David had put me in my place. Adrian did too.

If you are a reader of another set of beliefs, I hope you can tolerate so many Catholic stories. If it gets too thick, skip the story and go to another. You can always return if your curiosity or conscience get the best of you!

The Fighting Pastors – How To Petition To Oust Your Pastor

It was Friday, June 27tth, 1953, when I began my duties as assistant pastor of St. Mary's Church in Adrian. **Monsignor Breitenbeck** had taken me aside before I went there to tell me about the local "situation". He explained that there were two parishes in Adrian while the number of Catholics merited only one parish. However, over a hundred years ago, Adrian had many Catholic settlers, half of them Irish who brought their own priest with them and the other half German, who also had a German priest. So they started two rival parishes. They had been fighting each other ever since.

That year, a group of "modern" Catholics, who were members from both parishes, had petitioned **Edward Cardinal Mooney** to remove both of their pastors, **Father Sullivan** from St. Mary's and the pastor from St. Joseph's (whose name escapes me). They also requested the establishment of a new (third) parish on the west side of town where the new subdivisions were going up. Wisely, **Cardinal Mooney** agreed to their first request to replace the priests but not to their second. He assigned **Fr. Kerby** (Irish descent) to St. Mary's and **Father Bruck** (German descent) to St. Joseph's. Each parish had a very small high school and a grade school. They were instructed to unite their high schools and build a new high school on the grounds of St. Mary's.

Well, these two priests, egged on by some parishioners, could not get along. Father Bruck was jealous of St. Mary's which was a larger parish and had two priests. On top of that, the new high school was to be built – over there!

Monsignor Breitenbeck explained to me that I was to help bring things together. Sure.

Once **Father Bruck** found out I was the pastor's cousin, to say the least, it only made matters worse! Sure, they built the new Adrian Catholic Central, but by the end of my second year, both were petitioned out (again!) by the people and two new pastors were sent, both of German descent – **Father Shafer** to St. Mary's and **Father Kolb** to St. Joe's. They fought too. At the end of my third year in Adrian, **Father Charles Holton**, liked by everyone, was sent to St. Mary's and an equally likeable priest to St. Joe's.

I think I learned something through all this, though I'm not sure what. Some things for certain: people are fickle, priests are human, Christians (and, for that matter, Jews, Muslims, Hindus, etc.) need to practice what they preach and learn to get along with our fellow planet-dwellers. Funny thing, I liked all the priests and most of the people, even the man next door, and enjoyed being with them in Adrian.

One of my chief responsibilities in Adrian was to work with the Spanish-speaking population, which I will tell you more about later. I also served as the Athletic Director of the high school – which was enjoyable work – and religion teacher at the high school. My first year of teaching, whenever I couldn't handle a student, I had them leave the room and report to the principal's office. That happened probably over twenty times that first year. I taught in high school for a total of ten years, but that was the only year it was necessary to do that.

The reason I didn't need to keep sending students to the principal's office was that some of those great nuns taught me a "few tricks" about teaching (like listening to students' complaints) that made teaching a real joy to me. I later taught in Ecorse and then for four years at the Seminary. I did feel that students actually learned from my classes.

Back to Adrian..

Some Kerby-Van Antwerp History

I suppose, dear reader I owe you some background on **Father George Kerby**, my cousin and my first pastor in Adrian. He told me quite a bit of the old history of the family in Detroit.

Father Kerby's mother was a Van Antwerp, a sister of my great grandfather. She was well educated, while his father was not. His mother dominated the family and, as a result, Father Kerby forever remained a "mommy's boy", subservient to the wishes of women and deathly afraid of men. (I hate to say that, but it really was true, even though he was a very nice person.) Whenever things got "rough" in the parish (someone disagreed to his face about a decision) poor Father Kerby came back to the rectory and went to bed "sick" for a day or two. If something needed to be done, have a strong-minded woman ask him and he would readily agree, although silently resenting it. It was not the best way to run an organization.

Back to the history. According to Father Kerby, when **Francis Van Antwerp** died in 1889, he left the family farm in Grosse Pointe, on Jefferson near what is now the Grosse Pointe Yacht Club, to be divided among his descendents, the **Van Antwerps**, the **Kerbys** and the **Hickeys**. The Van Antwerps immediately sold their share of the farm since they were living in Detroit. The Hickeys and Kerbys held on to their property, subdivided it and made money. I suppose that's why there is a Kerby Road in Grosse Pointe and a Van Antwerp Street in Detroit. Father Kerby was still selling lots there while I was with him in the late '50s.

The Hickey descendents included **Monsignor Edward Hickey**, once Chancellor of the Archdiocese, pastor of St.

Mary's of Redford for many years and always known as a Detroit historian and art collector. Their descendents also included his brother who started the E. J. Hickey Men's Clothing store, first on Washington Boulevard and later in Grosse Pointe.

The Kerby family became famous too. Father Kerby's brother was a teacher, school principal and superintendent of schools in Grosse Pointe. There is even a school named after him. Another brother, a great golfer, became a golf pro at a country club in Akron, Ohio, living there until he died. He had a daughter, **Betty Kerby**, who became nationally know in women's professional golfing during the fifties.

Father Kerby was born and raised in a farm house near the old Van Antwerp farm house. He told me about the first time he met Dad. Dad was 18 and Father Kerby was about 8. Dad got off the old inner-urban railway near the Kerby farm and immediately started throwing stone at this Kerby boy. When the boy went home and told his mother about this big ugly kid who threw stones at him, his mother told him, "Don't worry, that's your cousin, **Gene Van Antwerp**". Dad, it turned out, was headed for a visit with his grandparents.

Old **Francis Van Antwerp** had a last name that the French-speaking farmers couldn't pronounce very well, so they just settled on calling him "Balentorp". They kidded him because all of his family was Catholic while he was a staunch Protestant. When he finally decided to become a Catholic, one of his friends said, "Mr. Balentorp, now that you're a Catholic, I suppose you must believe that all of your old Protestant friends, including your own parents, are going to hell?" Old Francis thought about the question, and not knowing all in "ins and outs" of what he was supposed to be believing, and not wanting to show he wasn't true to his new faith, he finally said, "Well, I guess you're right!" – At

least, this is the story as passed on to me by Father
Kerby.

My Dad told me of another wonderful custom the old
French farmers observed every Christmas Eve. Since
this was the one mass when they could eat and drink
before receiving Holy Communion (you had to fast from
Midnight from food and drink in those days), those
families that lived the farthest from the church started
early, usually on their horse drawn sled, and stopped at
the next house for a visit, food and drink. Together, these
families would head for the next house and again stop for
food and drink. And together, on to another house,
always joined by others. It was great neighborliness.
However, by the time some of them arrived at church,
there was evidence that they might have stopped at one
house too many. Or perhaps had one glass too many. As
a result, some sang too boisterly while others snored too
noisily at the evening's service. When I said, "wonderful
custom", I was referring to the "friendliness" of the
evening.

Priests never know what to do on New Year's Eve. My
priest friends generally played poker or bridge. But let me
tell you another story Father Kerby related about **Mike
Van Antwerp** and one of his brothers (whose first name
escapes me – he had three brothers, **Rufus, Charles
and James**) who were garbage collectors for many years
in Grosse Pointe. Neither brother had ever married. Both
lived with their widowed mother for many years; she
cooked, kept house, did their laundry, made their beds
and took care of them. She died when they were in their
late forties and they were lost. They became the family
"characters". They were noted for keeping any especially
good clothing that they found in the trash.

So when Father Kerby and four of his young priest
classmates stopped at their home on New Year's Eve in
1932, the brothers were already in bed. (I remember one

of his classmates that night was **Monsignor Flynn** who taught me Gregorian chant in the seminary.) When Mike came to the door very disheveled, he wanted to warn his brother to dress properly before coming downstairs. Mike kept pacing around the room, saying very loudly each time he passed the entrance to the stairs, "What a privilege to **have five priests** in the house". His brother finally came down, dressed in "long johns" and dressed in top hat and tails!

Now back to Adrian…and priestly duties

This is a photo of me at the altar,
taken by my classmate, Fr. Bob Zerafa

Saying Mass

There was something special and sacred about celebrating the holy sacrifice of the Mass. I was the human instrument used by God to recall the death of Christ on the cross – His sacrifice – by using the most common food elements used by humans, bread and wine, to become His Body and Blood. Christ foretold he would do this, i.e., give us His Body to eat and His Blood to drink. Many "found it hard to believe and walked no more with Him". The Apostles stuck with Him, trusting He would do it in a way that would not be gruesome but would demand our belief, our faith in Him.

I will always be amazed by God's ingenious ways. I know there is no "time" with Him and so the Death on the Cross and all the offerings of the "holy Sacrifice" of the Mass by all the priests of all time are as one moment with God.

Just amazing. Demands faith.

So, going to Mass will always be awesome to me. It matters little whether there are guitars, symphony orchestra, or no music at all. Or whether I like the priest or dislike him. Or if the sermon is good or not. Like going to the grocery store to get food, regardless of who the grocer is or how pretty the store's walls. It's the groceries I go for.

Same at church. The Mass will always be special and sacred to me. When I said Mass and now when I attend Mass, it is being with God, getting His "groceries" – the inspiring message of redemption and salvation, and the graces to carry on.

Well, that's off my chest! Now, you can relax, friend and think of lighter things.

Take Sex For Example

I never gave great sermons. I sure tried. My first sermon was frightening and I would have made it through all right if I hadn't spotted in the third row one of my St. Gregory High School archenemies from our teenage rivalry in neighborhood sports and fighting for parking lots. (we used neighborhood vacant lots to make money parking cars during events the the University of Detroit's stadium.) Is that **Jim Swoish**? What is HE doing here? – It turned out he was dating one of the **Jacobson girls** who had moved from Detroit to Adrian.

But we had received courses in public speaking all through the seminary. **Father Ed Majewski** taught us for several years. One thing he told us that was a real help was how to get our audience's attention when we started to lose it. Simply pause, a few seconds of silence, then in a booming voice, shout out, "TAKE SEX, FOR EXAMPLE!!"

It was a 12:30 p.m. Mass on a hot summer Sunday when I noticed that the St. Mary's parishioners were either resting their eyes or reading the *Michigan Catholic* or checking their fingernails. No one was listening. I paused. There was silence for a few moments. Then I said in a loud voice, "TAKE SEX FOR EXAMPLE!!!"

Everyone moved. "What did he say?" "Did I miss something?"

I had their attention. However, **Father Majewski's** advice didn't help me know how to fit it in with my subject, whatever that was. So the sermon ended shortly afterwards. But it did work! It sure woke the people up.

Migrants

Michigan in those days had 46,000 migrant farm workers. They came to pick our crops, including tomatoes, pickles, potatoes, sugar beets, cherries, apples and peaches. People tell me we still have a high number of migrants today. These workers arrived in late May and left when the frost hit about the first of October. They came mainly from Texas, Oklahoma, Arkansas, and Florida. In our area, they were found in Monroe, Lenawee and Hillsdale counties. More than half were Spanish-speaking Texans, displaced by the "mojados" (illegal "wetbacks" who waded the river) in their home towns. The others were mostly Blacks from the South who were really "conned" into coming for the "big money" up North. In the early days we had some "braceros" (literally, men with arms – meaning men who worked with their hands) directly from Mexico through an international agreement. In the Saginaw area, they had some Puerto Ricans flown in under a special contract with the Puerto Rican Department of Labor. Some other farm workers also came from the inner cities of Detroit and Toledo.

I was to help these migrants spiritually and materially. All told, I spent nine summers and learned a lot from them. I also did a study of their educational history and another study of their economic impact on our local economies. Let me tell you about these.

If I ever found a great small town, it is Blissfield, Michigan. The people there have always been great, from the **Al O'Mearas** to the car dealer; from the farmers to the members of the Kiwanis Club. I was fortunate to meet many of them while working with migrants in the area. **Sgt. Gill** from the State Police told me that they had fewer problems with migrants than with the local residents. The car dealer told me he made a lot of money every summer by selling every used car he had to them. I wondered if other local businesses also made money during those harvest periods.

So I went down the main streets from the Gambels store to the big grocery store, even the shoe store, asking questions. Everyone told me their sales went up considerably because the migrants bought food, clothing, and all kinds of goods in town. The manager of the Blissfield Bank estimated that they must have spent considerably over a million dollars every summer plus they made out many money orders for those who sent money back to family in Texas. So I learned how these hardworking, stoop laborers helped the city of Blissfield prosper! I was happy that the local citizens recognized this contribution and put on a yearly picnic for the farm workers.

A few years later, I sponsored a week-end retreat for teen aged migrants. The people from Erie, Michigan did the cooking. Speakers came to talk with these young people, including **Roger Playwin**, from the Monroe CYO (*Catholic Youth Organization*), someone from a labor union and someone from the Monroe County Health Department. (**Roger Playwin** went on to work with **Congressman Hertel** and at this writing runs the *Archdiocesan Council of the Society of St. Vincent de Paul.*)

In getting to know these young people, I discovered that most of them were either dropouts or considerably behind in school, because they missed so much school while on the road following the crops. I wrote the grade levels down for each of the fifty-some youngsters and noted that the highest grade reached by all but one was the 8th grade, and the average end of education was completion of the seventh grade. The following week, I took a census of their parents, most of whom were not migrants when they were young. I discovered that the parents averaged completion of the tenth grade! Their children, as migrants, were worse off educationally. What a waste!

There were many bad situations that I found distasteful. For example, I found a wonderful family eating "bread" they made from just flour and water to feed their children since they didn't have any money, because they arrived before the crops were ready for picking.

Another time, I picked up two 18 year old Black youths from Arkansas who were penniless and decided to hitchhike back home. (What nice kids they were, like my brother, Dan, I remember thinking.) They had been led to believe they would earn "lots of money" picking tomatoes in Michigan, so they signed up and rode "Big John's" bus to Monroe County. They had arrived two weeks before the "first picking" so they owed Big John for the ride up, and for each meal they ate. When they finally picked tomatoes the first day, as many and as fast as they could for almost twelve hours, they discovered someone had removed their number tags from the bushels they picked (usually replaced by that person's number) so they worked all day for nothing! One of them had even quit a gas station attendant job to come here! I felt so sorry for them, I gave them all the money I had with me and drove them to the Toledo bus station.

There were so many similar stories. And I wondered if anyone really knew the plight of these workers. Or even cared. I still wonder. Three cheers for saints like **Cesar Chavez!**

I knew that most of the farmers were good, hard working people. Many provided fairly decent cabins for their workers. It seemed that, if we could pay our workers more and let them rent their own housing, our system would be fairer. Much of our food costs are in packaging and transporting, not in wages. Excluding them from social security for the first few months of employment actually effectively excludes them from the retirement protection that most Americans enjoy. Like I say, my sermons never were that effective! I should have talked about real things like these.

The archdiocesan migrant program grew over the years. We had schools for migrant children, with college students from Marygrove and Sienna Heights Colleges teaching them. The big force to help were the women of the Archdiocesan Council of Catholic Women with people like **Hope Brophy**. They were assisted by the IHM nuns from Monroe and the Dominican nuns from Adrian. Eventually, there were medical clinics in Ida and Erie. We sponsored classes for the adults in auto mechanics, sewing and cooking with funds from the **Jerry McCarthy Foundation**.

Government, sometimes, does noble things. I was most impressed with our government when a young man, years later, came to see me and stated that **President John F. Kennedy** had authorized him to cut any and all red tape to help migrant farm workers. He asked what he could do to help. I told him that many migrants tried each year to stay up North with their families but usually failed because they couldn't find jobs. He told me that if I found families who wanted to quit the migrant stream, he would train them, provide them with housing and support during their training. Even better, he would assure them of full time employment once they finished training. I found eleven families. He got the Sisters of the Immaculate Heart of Mary to house them and provide classroom space at the Sister's Motherhouse in Monroe and he hired teachers. It worked. Not all, but several of those families were given a good start in life through that effort. I now have great confidence in what our government can do if it has the will to do it!

Knights of Columbus

In many ways, I was fortunate to be the only "assistant pastor" in any of the Catholic parishes in Lenawee County. It helped me when we formed young adults groups. It singled me out to be the messenger for most of the pastors to obtain their newly consecrated holy oils from the cathedral in Detroit every Holy Thursday. But it also made me eligible to be the chaplain for the Adrian Council of the Knights of Columbus. I enjoyed that because I liked the members there so much. I can't remember the Grand Knight's name, something like **"LeRoy" Smith**, but he was a winner, a wonderful man in every way. I explained to him that I would like to accept their invitation, but they had no Mexican-American members. I told him I would accept the post of chaplain as soon as they had several Hispanic members.

To my edification, their members went door to door and recruited enough members so that I would join. I was so proud of them. To have Hispanics as members of the Knights of Columbus, to me, was a signal of their further acceptance into the Catholic community as equals.

Marriages "in the Church" – iceboating friend

In those days, all of us had many prejudices that we inherited from our parents or peers. My Dad always liked Democrats more than Republicans, poorer people more than wealthy persons, veterans who had served overseas in battle more than non-veterans (or those who were MPs or in the Ordinance Corps), and, as Catholics, those who were married "in the Church" more than those Catholics whose marriage was not witnessed by a priest. I'm sure that I was exposed to many other biases that I even hesitate to mention but that were racial, religious or nationality based.

But, as a Catholic priest, I would be expected to help all Catholics remain in the good graces of the Church. This included helping those who had not been married "in the Church" receive this sacrament. Many of the Spanish-speaking, probably because of the scarcity of priests in Texas, had not been married by a priest. I was fortunate to be able to assist many couples to do this in Adrian, which probably looks strange in the marriage records of St. Mary's Parish since I'm sure I did over one hundred in those five years.

But I helped many "Anglos" (non-Spanish speaking) get married in the Church, too. I remember suggesting to one fellow who was not a Catholic that he was responsible for his wife not following her faith by his refusal to repeat his marriage vows in front of a priest. He got so mad he showed up that night at the rectory to tell me off. In return, I started yelling at him and really lost my temper and then I actually pushed him out of the door, effectively "throwing him out". An hour later, he returned to apologize about the same time as I was calmed down and feeling like a heel myself. From that point on we became very good friends. He and his wife repeated their vows in front of me and he introduced me to ice-boating on Devils Lake which we enjoyed together several times. Sometimes, it takes a little special event to really get to know and appreciate another human being. Within a year, my new friend was called by God to his reward and he's probably up there laughing as I write this!

"Call 319J"

Using a telephone in Adrian in 1953 was similar to the how it was when I was a small boy in Detroit. It was before telephones with dials. You cranked a bell handle on the side, got the operator's attention and asked for a number like 319J. I felt like I had gone back in time when I moved to Adrian.

But not for long. Modern life hit Adrian like a storm when the General Telephone Company took over that same year. We had real numbers, long ones; we had dial phones!! We were big-time!

Unfortunately, it took a while for neighboring areas to catch up. I remember calling Deerfield, Michigan and asking for the parish phone number. An operator said, "You looking for **Father Griffith**? I just saw him walk into the grocery store across the street. Why don't you call him in about an hour?"

I had to laugh, too, when I wanted to talk to a parishioner whose mailing address was in Cadmus, Michigan. They also had a small independent telephone company operated in someone's front room. I called the Cadmus Telephone Company and asked for the **Marvin** family. The operator, a man, informed me that that family was a General Telephone Company customer and gave me their number. Then he added, "Anytime the Cadmus Telephone Company can assist the General Telephone Company, just let us know!"

Sports – Athletic Director; Soccer Coach

One of my responsibilities in Adrian was that of Athletic Director for our high school. That meant watching its income and expenses, using many volunteer coaches scheduling games, buying uniforms, but, most of all, having a great time with the kids. At that time, we belonged to the "Little Six" League which included the public high schools from the towns of Sand Creek, Ida, Deerfield, our school (first, St. Mary's, then, Adrian Catholic Central) and Britton and Cadmus – high schools that were real power houses. The "biggies" like Adrian, Morenci, Hudson, Blissfield and Clinton were too much for us.

I had great respect for the coaches and athletic directors of those high schools. They were all dedicated men, shaping the character of so many youths, like the dedicated people who are the teachers and coaches in all the small towns and in the big cities of our country. They were so considerate of the kids in all the sports. I saw this when we got together to choose the "All League Teams" in each sport, when the kids would get their names in the paper for the first or second team or for "honorable mention". They'd look at our kids – **Bob Saks**, **Tom**

Hirons, **Tom Kirkwood**, **Bill Carey**, for example, and say, "We need someone from each school for the first team, and the second team and a couple for honorable mention". Before this, I innocently thought that all-star teams were picked scientifically!

Being Athletic Director was work, and, like all work, it has fun, enjoyable sides and tougher, more unpleasant sides. One of the parishioners controlled the "Athletic Fund" most of which came from money raised by ticket sales at football and basketball games, from selling refreshments, and from fundraisers like the annual sports dinner and car washes. It was used for various expenses including sports equipment. When I arrived, the person in charge of that fund had no idea how much money was in it. I told him I was taking over, so he gave me some cash. It might have been correct but how would anyone ever know? I'm not sure that I was any better than him at the sports finances, but at least I had a record.

For many private religious schools, money has always been difficult. You had to depend upon the contributed efforts of many volunteer workers and coaches. In Adrian we had many wonderful persons who gave of themselves to help the young men and women in sports. Names like **Ed Stepansky**, **Sack** and **Sacksteder**, **Jack McAdam**, **Bob Westfall**, and many others come back to me. We owe them very much. When our high school was accredited through the wonderful efforts of **Sr. Ann Patricia, O.P.**, it was necessary to hire a coach who was a credentialed teacher of physical education. This was a most difficult task, to tell those who had given so much time as volunteer coaches that we could not hire them.

I had a bright idea that might help improve relationships between the "German" parish and our "Irish" parish when we opened the joint new high school. It was a fact that some people resented the fact that our teams were still called "The Fighting Irish". (It received this name when it was St. Mary's High School and had received Notre Dame University's old football uniforms.) I impulsively decided, crazily, on my own initiative, to change its name to "**The Aztecs**", thinking it could also serve to attract some Spanish-speaking athletes. Once this news appeared in *The Adrian Telegram's* Sports Section, the kids in the school next door (those Adrian High School kids were always sharp!) immediately substituted two "s"s for the "z" and razzed our kids all day!

I called the reporter and explained the problem. He wrote the smoothest retraction you could ever find that appeared the following day. Ever since then, I have had the greatest admiration for writers and reporters and what they can do with words!

We also had a football program for our seventh and eighth grade students. However, one day, the athletic director of Sand Creek Grade School called and wanted his 7th and 8th graders to play our kids in soccer. It had to be soccer because they couldn't afford football uniforms. (And I always had thought public schools had lots of money!) I needed a sport activity for our 5th and 6th graders so I told him our younger kids would beat his older kids.

Remembering how I watched soccer so often in Mexico, I figured one of the Latino men in Adrian would be delighted to coach a soccer team with our 5th and 6th graders. Wrong! Adrian Latinos were pure Americans and only knew football, baseball and basketball.

So I outfitted our youngsters in baseball socks, and high school basketball shorts and sleeveless numbered shirts. With a "How to Play Soccer" book in one hand, I coached and our team played them in three games. Lost all three. But Sand Creek only scored 1 goal in the last game and our youngsters thought of that as a real victory! That was in 1957. We gave up soccer after that.

The Legions of Mary and the Society of St. Vincent de Paul

The *Legion of Mary* was an active group that met weekly, prayed together, reflected on spiritual growth and did home visiting to help parishioners spiritually. It is very similar to the *Society of Saint Vincent de Paul* with the major difference being the kind of help given. The Vincentians do home visiting to help any persons materially and spiritually.

In Adrian we had both organizations. The *St. Vincent de Paul Conference* was headed by **Bob Hayes** who ran the Florsheim shoe store. **Dr. Ed Schmidt**, my dentist, was a member. Others included **Duke Piotter** who ran a grocery with the best meats in town, **Ed Jacobson** who was a plant manager in a local factory and a "neat" man whose name I've forgotten (but not his smiling face nor the story of how he got a job by telling the personnel interviewer that he was an "experienced buffer"). **Bob Hayes** used to laugh when he told the story of when he first joined the Society of St. Vincent de Paul in the Depression era. A farmer asked them to buy him a horse so he could plow his fields. Being "city" boys, they bought the best horse they could for $15. The horse died of a heart attack after the first day of plowing. So much for good intentions!

The Legion of Mary was more focused on spiritual needs. (I would like to think that's why I gave it more time and not because there were more females involved!) They did so much to help people. It kept growing in numbers of members until we had five groups – including a Spanish-speaking group and a teen-age group. **Emma Marvin**, **Mrs. Jacobson**, **Virginia Schmidt**, **Frances Hutchinson**, **Blanca Cuevas** and many other dedicated women helped people and the parish in a thousand ways!

The Art of Hearing Confessions – But Don't Let A Drunken Man Sit On Your Lap

The sacrament of Penance, or Confession, is something that has always amazed me. It really shows how smart God is. We humans, with few exceptions, have weak, even sinful moments. Sometimes we regret them for years as their memories come back to "haunt" us. If only they could be erased, completely forgiven, we could more easily be at peace.

God evidently knew this and left us a way to release our guilts, feel forgiven, and even get advice from a person trained in spiritual guidance. In a sense, Catholics who use this sacrament wisely, should be able to be at peace with themselves, have more self-confidence, be better persons. I always wondered if we would need as many psychiatrists if more people could avail themselves of the grace of this sacrament. However, knowing something about mental illness, I realize there will also always be a need for good psychiatrists!

So, on the human, sinner aspect of confession, I think it is wonderful, a real plus in the Catholic and Lutheran traditions. (Check your Lutheran catechism and see how similar their explanation of public and private confession is to that of Catholics.)

It is different on the human side of hearing confessions. In my days of hearing confessions, it was like being locked in a small, dark closet, sometimes for hours on end, while fellow humans, young and old, told you their most innermost secrets and failings. Try as I might to listen patiently and to give spiritual guidance, I know I failed from time to time. Even fell asleep (please don't reveal this!).

I do remember a person coming in and instead of confessing, merely told me that she thought the other priest was dead – she got no response when she confessed. I figured he was asleep so I just said, "Knock loud on the wall of the confessional and see what happens!" He was okay, i.e., he woke up.

During the 2:30 a.m. Mass at Most Holy Trinity, while hearing confessions, I realized that the sermon by **Father Grace Agius, CSB,** ended very abruptly. Shortly after that, in the middle of hearing someone's confession, the door to my section opened and a very drunken man entered, sat on my lap and shut the door behind him. I just pushed him up and I got out, and opened the door. There appeared two ushers to guide him towards the door. Father Agius filled me in later, the poor fellow had come up in front of him while he preached, stood directly in front of him, perhaps three feet away, and mimicked every gesture that poor Father Agius used until he just stopped preaching. You'd have to hear and see Father Agius describe this with his own gestures!

There was always something special about this sacrament in the effect that it had on me personally. The very sacredness of it awed me. I could never break that "seal of confession" by revealing, in any way, matter that was confessed to me. Beyond that, it revealed to me the sinfulness and weakness inherent in every person and the need for strengthening, supporting, reinforcing and helping our fellow humans.

I remember being surprised (and I should not have been) to find in hearing confessions in other countries, even in remote sections of Brazil and Mexico, that people committed to same kinds of sins. Children still disobeyed, adults everywhere were victims of greed and lust and anger. Men, women, Blacks, Anglos, Latinos, transvestites and those of varying sexual orientation --- humans, all of us, struggling to be better persons.

It somehow made me more tolerant of others, more willing to understand them and to be of help. And, it brought out the fact that there are a lot of "saints". There is goodness in every person, even those I would otherwise think of as "bad" persons. From then on, I would extend **Father Flanagan's** famous words "*There is no such thing as a bad boy*" to most of the people in the world. You can see how this sacrament of penance is awe inspiring and humbling to the priest who hears confession. Only God could think up such a thing as the sacrament of penance.

Special People In Adrian

There were many people in Adrian that I liked. As a matter of fact I think I liked every one of them. I can't mention them all, but let me tell you about a few of them.

Bob Hayes, as I mentioned above, ran the Hayes Florsheim Shoe Store. He was a wonderful man who gave free shoes to every priest and to many poor persons! (And, of course, since the shoes were free, these people kept returning!) I only took one pair from Bob because I didn't want to hurt his business. (Although he sent me a second pair when he figured those had worn out.) In all my life, I don't think I have ever met a kinder man.

Aunt Maggie Hayes was Bob Haye's maiden aunt who lived in an apartment above the shoe store on Main Street. She was ninety years old when I arrived and ninety-five when I left Adrian. I found her to be a delight and still a little devilish! She sure liked to kid around.

If you know anyone with diabetes, you will enjoy this other story about Aunt Maggie. She had diabetes. She couldn't eat sweets. But she liked sweets. About once a month, the bakery (which was also under her apartment) would deliver a lemon meringue pie to me, with one piece missing. Dear old Aunt Maggie, in her cute, devilish way, would order a pie for me but ask the bakery to stop by her apartment before they delivered it. There she removed one piece for herself. Bob Hayes paid her bills, but her bakery bill simply showed the monthly delivery of lemon pies to Father Van Antwerp. Think he knew?

In preparation for building the new Adrian Catholic Central High School, we tore down a small brick building next door to the house where **Carl and Betty Koenig** lived. (He was the parish's dependable, overworked, and underpaid maintenance man.) The "shed" had been the original church, later the parish one-room school, then, in turn, the parish hall, the pastor's garage, and finally, just a storage shed. What a history it could tell, if it only could speak. But speak it did: In tearing down the old building, under the flooring, the construction men found school children's papers in perfect condition dating in the 1800's. One paper bore the name of Margaret Hayes, grade four, and a date in 1872! Can you imagine? I showed it to Father Kerby and then took the paper to Aunt Maggie. What a piece of history! I wonder if anyone kept that paper since I left it with her.

Ed Stepansky was an extraordinarily dedicated man who helped make the high school athletic program successful and whom I never really properly thanked. (We were told in the seminary to stop having contact with former parishioners when we left an assignment so that the new priest would have a free hand. I tried to conform to this inhuman practice at least in some measure. I regret that now.) Ed ran a bar and grill restaurant on Main Street called Mr. Ed's. He also was raising a wonderful family. Yet Ed found time to help me with the athletic program, probably giving ten hours or more a week to it, especially during football season. Now that I am married and understand family obligations, I wonder how many good people I imposed on, as I must have done with Ed. At this point, I can best repay him by saying a prayer for him from time to time.

"Duke" Piotter ran a local butcher shop and grocery store. He was a real "man's man". I liked Duke a lot. He helped me on most of the athletic programs and helped the parish in many other ways. He had become a convert to Catholicism and many of his relatives resented it at the time. That resentment was hard on Duke. I certainly hope his family got over it before his untimely death prior to age fifty. I recall how he helped me pull a trick on our French-Canadian housekeeper at Christmas in 1956.

Rudy Salazar, was a strapping six-foot-two, handsome Latino who was married to **Doris Trevino.** Rudy was the son-in-law of the distinguished **Ignacio Trevino** who looked like he owned all of Mexico, and carried himself in the same way. But Ignacio, probably 80 years old at the time, came to every Latino meeting I held. Rudy brought him. The two of them made my work easy since they were respected by every Latino in town. Rudy became my "right hand man" and helped get other workers for me like **the Garcia brothers, Armando, Arnulfo, and Arturo**, and men like **Calistro Torres** and **Luis Gonzalez**. I owe a lot to Rudy and Doris. I felt like crying with happiness when I saw them at a Latino dinner in Detroit in 2002 when their son**, Ignacio Salazar**, was honored by the Latino community.

You'd want to know more about **Luis Gonzalez**, a delightful Puerto Rican from the west coast of the island. Luis would still be there if he hadn't won a hundred dollars in the check pool while working in the Coca Cola bottling plant. With the special rate of $45 he flew to New York City, only to have so many Puerto Ricans tell him there was no work there. Somehow (this had to be a real blessing!) someone told him to take a bus to Adrian, Michigan because there were jobs there. He didn't know where Adrian was (see, there are lots of people who don't know where it is!) but he came to town. In Adrian, he met a wonderful woman, **Maria Saenz**, who had been widowed with four children when **Pedro Garcia**, with too much tequila, shot and killed him. Luis eventually married Maria, became active in the parish and served as "rector" of the Cursillo in Spanish for many years. We all admired him!

Pancho Villa

I should also say a word about **Gregorio Aranda**. He had to be the oldest Latino in Adrian, or one of the oldest. Gregorio told me wonderful stories of the old days. He had been a member of **Pancho Villa's** army during the Mexico revolution (1910-20). He told me how you could see the cannon balls coming during the battles and how they ran to avoid them. Those cannonballs did not explode; but were big, iron, black baseballs that could put a hole right through you. With my background viewing movies of modern warfare and exploding shells, to hear his stories made history come alive and be real to me. Gregorio told me that, when Pancho Villa was paid off in gold after the revolution, he assembled his troops in Vera Cruz, where he supposedly was going to pay them from the gold he received. Gregorio, however, was called away because his uncle was dying. When he returned, the whole army of Pancho Villa had set sail and left port, never to be heard of again. It was rumored that Pancho Villa had chosen to send them to sea and sink the ships so that he would not have to pay them. Whether that story was true or not, Gregorio never went looking for Pancho Villa to seek his back pay. But he came up to the States just to be safe.

Tom Kirkwood was a senior in high school when I first met him. His mother was president of the St. Mary's Rosary Altar Society and was active in the "LCBA" – the Ladies Christian Benevolent Society. His father was an exemplary man respected by everyone. Tom was still an altar boy. He had a sister, Judy, and a younger brother, Dennis. Tom was co-captain of both the football and the basketball team. I taught Tom religion and threw him out of class a few times for failure to have his homework done on time. But he grew up. He entered the seminary and accompanied me on one of my many trips to Mexico. Today, we remain good friends. Tom has served as one of the outstanding Archdiocesan high school principals for over twenty-five years, working at Shrine High School in Royal Oak. He has a wonderful wife, Mary, and three children, Pat, Mike and Kathy. Their home is just 8 houses away from our home.

Calvin Beaubien was a young married man who worked at the Standard gas station at the corner down the street in Adrian. "Cal" took care of my car better than anyone ever did, before or since those days. He was the kind of upstanding young man you'd hope your daughter would someday marry. I liked him. Some years ago I heard that he had purchased his own gas station and was doing well. It made me feel good.

Don Dunmore was a newcomer to town, a young man who took over a funeral home. His friendly manner and parish involvement brought many Catholic funerals to his place. His wife was active in the Lutheran parish, which,

I'm sure, helped Don be able to provide his services to many Lutherans as well. They were a great couple.

Jack McAdam was another young man that I liked. For many years he helped run the athletic program. I think he was hurt when we couldn't hire his friend, Jack Condon, who had been a volunteer coach for several years. McAdam quit helping the program. I still liked him and appreciated his work and his loyalty to his friend.

Tom Hirons was a student in our high school and good scholastically and in sports. I can still visualize his left-handed bullet passes right into the stomachs of our receivers as our quarterback. I also marveled at his left handed basketball shots whizzing through the net without touching the rim. Tom was the quarterback of our football team the year we won the Little Six championship. You probably read about that! After graduation, Tom went to Notre Dame University and graduated in nuclear physics. I never heard of him again.

I probably shouldn't own up to this: Tom's parents sent me a Christmas card without a stamp and I had to pay three cents "postage due". I promptly sent them a Christmas card, with no return address. Without a stamp!

Bill Carey also was one of our students. He later married **Nancy Darling** who was in the same class. (I used to love calling on Nancy in class when I taught her; I would call her fist name, then pause, and say her last name softly! – just fun!) I had a phone call one day from the Track Coach of Hudson High School. He asked me if we had a track team and I said, "No!" Then he told me that he had been coaching track for fifteen years and he had a student who was transferring to our school that was the fastest track runner he ever saw. His advice was that we start a track team. I thanked him and we started a track team. It only lasted two years until Bill graduated. But in those two years, we won all kinds of ribbons at local, regional and state-wide track meets, thanks to Bill Carey, a delightful young man who led our team to glory! Bill became a fireman in Adrian and since that was almost 45 years ago, he must be thinking of retiring inside of a few years.

Father George Gaynor Was For Real

Another priest that I grew to admire greatly was **Father George Gaynor**. When I knew him, he served as chaplain both at the Girls' Training School and the Dominican Sisters' Motherhouse, both in Adrian, Michigan, each dealing with females whose life experiences differed greatly. George had his "feet on the ground" and could handle any tough problem with tactful diplomacy and solid advice.

George told me to always be nice to pregnant unmarried girls. He explained that the girls who were real "pros" in matters of sex rarely got pregnant and if they did, they arranged for abortions pretty quick, legally or illegally. But the really nice girls, the innocent girls, were the ones who were pregnant and unmarried. From that day on, whenever a single girl told me she needed help because she was pregnant, I went out of my way to help her as best I could.

One summer, I had a beautiful young woman, about twenty-one, tell me that she wanted to escape from her father who had been having incest with her since she was nine years old. I asked George's help and he got her a job at St. John's Hospital in Detroit. I drove her into Detroit, the nuns found her a place to live and it almost worked. Until she got "lonesome" for her Dad!

When the Lenawee County Health Department was about to take a malnourished child away from its parents, George helped again. He got St. John's to keep the baby for two months until it was strong and healthy. I picked it up and brought it back to its parents, with plenty of food and a whole wardrobe of clothing donated by the nurses of St. John's Pediatric Division. (I could write about many things St. John's Hospital did to help the people I worked with. The hospital and its staff were great!)

I don't think Father Gaynor ever became as well known as **Monsignor Clement Kern**. But he was every bit as good and as involved with the poor as Father Kern was. Since I faced a lot of jealous bickering as I listened to the priests I was first stationed with, it was so relaxing and enjoyable to spend a little time, now and then, with a real solid man like Father George Gaynor!

The Nuns Are Real People

With so many of my relatives who were nuns, you'd think I would know more about their humanness. I suppose I really didn't see them often enough to judge that side. I saw them more during visiting hours or at family gatherings.

Now, however, I was working with nuns frequently and I came to know many of them and appreciate them as individual persons, with good points and bad sides, with multiple or with limited talents, creativity, virtues, and intelligence. My experience of working with nuns was enlightening, scandalous and awe-inspiring. I saw them at their best and sometimes at their worst. Did you know that nuns get angry? Jealous? Even petty? It took me a while to remember that only a limited number of humans lived free of sin, therefore even saints were sinners, from time to time.

There is something wonderful about a calling to the religious life and its vows of poverty, chastity, and obedience. It is one of the miracles of our faith that thousands of men and women throughout the world live their lives dedicated to the service of their God and their fellow human beings in such fields as education, health care, social services and the spiritual, contemplative life. You and I can list countless examples of such persons, including people like Mother Teresa, for example.

The miracle is not just that they give of themselves so completely in a noble calling, but I really believe that it is miraculous that so many varied persons, with different tastes and distinct temperaments, can continue to live and work together in community life! That takes guts, dedication and the idealism that motivates individuals to greatness.

The Saints:

I have always been impressed by those who really were "holier than" me. Often these were simpler people of great faith and hearts of gold, but who were poor and even uneducated. I met so many wonderful people in the hills of Mexico, Brazil and the Dominican Republic and some very special people living on Detroit's Skid Row. Let me tell you, it is scary and totally humbling to be a "holy" Catholic priest and meet so many who put you to shame in their generosity, prayerfulness and kindness!

I can't tell you about all of them, but let me tell you about a lady named **Wilma Senour**.

I had seen her before. In church, I think. But I never met her until this April day in 1954 when I answered the doorbell for the rectory office on Division Street. She was middle aged, small of build, and looked up at me as if frightened. She wanted to talk to a priest and I was the only one around.

We sat down in my office and she told me her story. She had moved to Adrian from Illinois. She was the Director of Nursing at the old Bixby Hospital and she was assistant pastor of the Church of the Nazarene. She was also the secretary for the Lenawee County Council of Churches. She spent an hour or two in prayer every day and time in reading and contemplating on God's word in the scriptures. Since her church was a ways away (near the Adrian airport), she found it convenient to spend her lunch period in St. Mary's church. St. Mary's was so close to the old hospital and always open. She often wondered, she said, why she found our church to be so conducive to prayer. Then one day she read a pamphlet from the back of the church on "the Real Presence" of Christ in the Eucharist. It explained how Christ is present in the host which was kept in the tabernacle in every Catholic church. His presence is always signified by a red vigil candle burning nearby.

So that was it! God is really present here in a very special way, she knew! But, if this is true, as she now believed, what does this mean to her years of protestant upbringing and beliefs? The trauma was increased by her standing as a minister. What would she tell the congregation and the pastor?

So here she was. She didn't ask me to help her through her trauma. She asked me two things: To instruct her in Catholic teachings so that she could enter the Catholic Church and to be her spiritual director so that she could lead a holy life!

Wow! I had instructed many people before her and after her in the teachings and practices of the Catholic faith. But no one, before or since, had ever asked me to lead them to holiness!

For the next four years, we met almost weekly. Darn her, she was reading deeper spiritual books, finding out how the saints had received spiritual direction and she wanted similar guidance from me. Geez, all I can say is that I did the best I could. I checked into all the best religious books and got advice from older priests. But I felt like a

Keystone Cop trying to show Mother Theresa the path to holiness.

Wilma Senour became involved in everything she could in the parish. She told me before I left in 1958 that she had cancer and she died about a year later. She would have made a great Catholic priest if that could have been possible. She did become a finer, holier person than anyone I met before or since!

There were many other saints in that city, not all were Catholics (I learned that from Wilma Senour!). There were **the Jacobsons, the Linehans, Dr. Sarapo and others**. I could go on but there is so much to share with you!

Starting A Credit Union

People, who have little resources and not much access to bank loans and credit, need to band together and form cooperatives for purchasing, saving money, getting loans and even housing. So I talked to **Father Clement Kern** of Most Holy Trinity Parish in Detroit to find out how we could start a credit union. Leave it to him. The next thing I knew, we were helped by an expert. **Don Murray** of *Ferndale Credit Union* (now called *Credit Union One*) came every Sunday for ten weeks to instruct the Latinos in Adrian on how to start and operate a Credit Union. We named it the *"Holy Family Credit Union"* (which I thought was a clever way to unite the ideals of the two parishes – St. Joseph's and St. Mary's). I wrote two pages of "By-Laws" on my typewriter at midnight so it could be approved. **Roberto Trevino** – a great young man who just finished high school – agreed to be our treasurer (the real big job in a credit union!). Bob later became the Lenawee County Treasurer.

The credit union dissolved a few years after I left there. That was a disappointment to me. However, I did start a credit union in the Dominican Republic a few years later which is still operating! Win a few, lose a few...

Braceros In Hudson

Let me explain how I discovered the "braceros".

I was appointed "confessor" for the nuns who staffed the Catholic school in Hudson, Michigan, about 15 miles west of Adrian (for those of you who were never residents of Lenawee County). At that time, confessors were appointed for each convent and they had to go there weekly and give the sisters the opportunity to confess their sins to a priest that was not working in the same parish. I enjoyed going there weekly, especially if I could get a young boy like **Mike Linehan** to keep me company. I usually bribed him with an ice cream cone.
(Today, amid the scandals I have read about, I think I'd be afraid to ask a youngster to go with me!!)

One summer day, I am driving through Hudson towards the church when I notice a large number of Latinos in the back of a truck. As they passed the Catholic church, they all took off their "sombreros" in true Latino respect for the house of God, putting them back on after they passed. Having gone often to Mexico, I recognize this as a cultural habit of "real" Mexicans, not the Tex-Mex brand of American born and bred Latinos. I asked about them.

The pastor told me that there were about eighty men from Mexico living a block away at the pickle factory.

The "Bracero" program started during World War II when the Texas and California growers couldn't get sufficient farm workers to harvest their crops. All the young men had gone into military service. The United States government made an agreement with Mexico so that Mexico would send farm workers to our country to pick our crops. In 1942, the United States signed the Bracero Treaty which reopened the floodgates for legal immigration of Mexican laborers. Between the period of 1942 and 1964, millions of Mexicans entered the U.S. as "braceros" under the Bracero Program to work temporarily under contract to United States growers and ranchers.

Under the Bracero Program, more than 4 million Mexican farm workers came to work the fields of the United States during this 22 year program. Impoverished Mexicans fled their rural communities and traveled north to work as braceros. It was mainly by the Mexican labor that America became the lushest agricultural center in the world.

So here I was, a block away every week. Thus it was easy for me for two summers to assist their spiritual needs. I regularly visited the Braceros, held services in Spanish for them, heard their confessions and helped them feel like they   were welcomed.

Little did I know how sometimes they were cheated out of their hard earned wages, not necessarily by their employer, but often by the local Latinos hired to supervise and to feed them.

Under the international agreement, workers who felt they were unjustly treated could register a complaint with the local U. S. Department of Labor office which would be investigated by them as soon as possible. Sure! Sounds nice on paper. In reality, not one Bracero knew the process nor how to access it. And, the Labor Department office was in Cleveland for the Midwest Region, and they only had three investigators for the six states. On top of this, any worker that was complaining too much, was simply put on a plane and sent back to Mexico.

I decided to beat the system when several men told me the specifics of how badly they were treated. I wrote a nasty letter to the Labor Department, directly to the senior investigator (Father Kern gave me his name and address). I sent the letter special delivery with receipt requested. The inspector was in Hudson in three days. The next thing I knew, the pickle factory was closed. I never asked how or why. I did feel terrible that the men had lost their jobs.

Forsthoefels Built A Bomb Shelter

The **Forsthoefel family** was one of the best – real class! Mr. Forsthoefel had a brother who was a Jesuit priest teaching at the University of Detroit. His daughter was Lenawee County's Sesquicentennial Queen. Mrs. Forsthoefel was an officer in the Rosary Altar Society of the parish.

But these were the days when we were all being told that the Russians might bomb us and we needed to be prepared. Facilities containing ground to air ballistic missiles were built around every major city in the United States. My dad showed me on a map where they were around Detroit, in Southfield, in Grosse Ile and elsewhere.

The Forsthoefels built a new home, with everything –
even a bomb shelter with sufficient supplies to last until
the end of the bombing, whenever that might be.

I wonder, every so often, whatever happened to the
bomb shelter?

Mother Gerald And The Dominican Motherhouse

No one can talk about the Adrian of "those days" without
recalling **Mother Gerald Barry, O.P.**, the *Mother General*
of the Adrian Dominican sisters. Mother Gerald had every
bit of the strong will and dominance of a "general" and
slightly less of motherly graces.

I liked Mother Gerald. I guess I liked her for the fact that
she got things done! I was working with some priests
(especially Father Kerby and to some extent, Father
Schaefer) who were so indecisive that it was nice to see
someone who made decisions!

There are many stories I could tell you about Mother
Gerald. I won't. Just know that God sends certain
persons here to accomplish certain things and leave it at
that. Some thought of her as too much of a dictator.
Fortunately, I did not work under Mother Gerald.

But the Mother House, under her direction, was a great
blessing to Adrian! Great women serve there as religious
dedicated to serve God and God's people. The sisters
from the motherhouse helped me constantly in my work
with the Hispanic community, both the residents and the
migrants, for which I am always grateful. Some of the
nuns would come to our church to go to confession when
they felt the need to go to confession to a stranger. For
that purpose, I served as an outside advisor. Hope I
helped.

Towns Around Adrian: Morenci, Sand Creek, Blissfield, Deerfield, Tecumseh

I would love to take you, dear reader, on a tour of the towns around Adrian. For the sophisticated urbanites of Toledo and Detroit and Jackson and Ann Arbor, these towns are "off the beaten path". But let me tell you, the people in them are the nicest, most cordial and neighborly folks you'd meet in a long time. The high school is the center of all the social life not found in the churches. There isn't much crime, violence, drugs, or even drunkenness. Those (few!) that are sinners generally visit the urban areas (you don't drink in Riga, Michigan!) so life is simpler and more pleasant. Even the restaurants are wonderful, though fewer in number.

There is nothing like a hot fudge sundae in Morenci after the local high school football game, or relaxing dinner at the restaurant in Blissfield to finish off a hard week.

The Late Father Dominic Foley

What can I say about "Dom"? He became one of the best known "characters" in the history of the Detroit diocesan clergy. Friendly as could be. Delightful to be with. But never rely on him for anything or think he might arrive on time!

Dom was appointed pastor for Hudson, Michigan, so we all knew that Lenawee County was to be cut out of the Detroit archdiocese. (When a "cut" was imminent, bishops often would assign priests they could do without to parishes in the areas to be cut.) In one parish, he contracted to have the interior of the church painted, got mad at the painters, and left the scaffolding up in the church for three years! Christmas celebrations, weddings, funerals – they all had taken place between the scaffolding.

Dom preached long sermons, as if the audience knew nothing and he had to start with Adam and Eve. Parishioners from Hudson would drive all the way to Adrian for Mass and get home before the sermon in Hudson was ended.

But the folklore was true about his <u>longest</u> sermon since he told me this himself. While he was serving as the pastor of Milford, Michigan, a funeral procession was coming up the church steps when it came to him that he had forgot to tell the janitor to dig the grave in the nearby parish cemetery. He quickly got in touch with the janitor and told him to dig a grave and he would preach until the janitor waved in the rear of the church. That would be the signal the grave was ready.

Well, it was winter. Middle of February. The ground was frozen like rock. I don't know how long the sermon was, but Dom told me it was the longest he ever gave!

Now you know.

Religious in our family

Previous page: Some of the family members in religious life in 1961, left to right: Sr. Dacia Van Antwerp, RSCJ, Sr. Mary Gertrude McDevitt, RSM, Sr. Dolores Van Antwerp, RSCJ, Sr. Anna Van Antwerp, RSCJ, Fr. Francis F. Van Antwerp, Eugene I. Van Antwerp, Mrs. Eugene I. (Frances McDevitt) Van Antwerp, Fr. Thomas J. Van Antwerp, Fr. George H. Kerby, Fr. John G. Van Antwerp, Fr. George B. Van Antwerp, Fr. Eugene I. Van Antwerp, SS. (Missing are Fr. George Reno, SJ, Sr. Annetta McDevitt, IHM, Sr. Mary Arthur (Ellen) Van Antwerp, IHM, Sr. Francis Marion Van Antwerp, OP., and Fr. Tom McDevitt)

Help From Lutheran Pastor To Get Government Food

The local Lutheran pastor and I had a loud public argument at a meeting in the Adrian City Hall. It was over a film at the local drive-in theater that was "Condemned" by the Catholic dominated Legion of Decency.

Today, I would control my anger. But I was young and brash. I was ashamed later. What made matters worse is that the Lutheran pastor was the only person in town that knew how to get federal money and surplus food. He was receiving it for his church school.

I called him. He was so friendly and nice when I went over. He explained everything and even gave me the forms to get me started.

He proved the strength of ecumenism before the Vatican Council ever used the word.

The Trio In Rural Poverty – Past Petersburg

The beauty of ministry is that every day is different. Not at all boring like an assembly line.

On the first Friday of every month, I took Holy Communion to about fifteen home-bound sick persons in the parish. At a farm house near Petersburg, dusty and dirty and so cluttered that I had to walk in aisles of old newspapers and trash, there lived three "saints" that many people would find repulsive. The old whiskered man in the bed with the shotgun within his reach looked filthy, mean and frightening. His sister, much cleaner, was crippled by a back problem that made her walk with her head near the floor. The youngest brother was mentally challenged and didn't talk, although he seemed to understand when spoken to. He served as the errand person for them. He walked about ten miles each way to go to town for groceries and other needs. They lived off a very small income from one social security check. They were really poor!

They were always astoundingly pleasant and nice. When I would arrive, the challenged younger man would meet me with a candle and each would await me in a different room so they would have privacy for confessions. I think I brightened their lives just a bit every month.

The Lenawee County Health Department contacted me to help them convince the three of them to enter the county home where they would get some health care and improved cleanliness in their daily lives, baths, clean sheets, clean clothes, good food. How we did this would make an interesting television show. At the time, it took lots of words and a ride in an ambulance that was not scheduled for a round trip.

The only one who objected loudly, was the oldest, bed-ridden brother. It took two months before he decided he liked it there. I brought them Communion many times after that to the county home. I could see that they finally enjoyed it – having a clean place to stay, receiving good care and food. I knew then that we had done the right thing.

Who Put A Smoke Bomb In Fr. Van's Engine?

Respect. That's important. Right?

Would you put a smoke bomb in Bishop Sheehan's car? In Martin Luther King Jr.' s car? Out of respect, you would demur.

So if I ever find out for sure that it really was **Tom Kirkwood**, today the loved and respected principal of Shrine High School, that put the smoke bomb in my car that night in Adrian.....

Thomas P. Kirkwood
Vice - President

(He has an honest face)

It Was Hard To Leave Adrian

Enough about Adrian. I loved being there and loved the people. They threw a good-bye party for me five days before I left. Hardly anyone came around during those five days. I packed my few belongings which fit nicely in my car. (Associate pastors didn't earn enough to own a lot of things in those days.) I cried as I drove northward out of town. I didn't see one person I knew that I could wave at.

Boy, How I Loved Ecorse

I hate to admit that I got lost finding my second assignment – Ecorse.

I'm coming in on the Ford Expressway (I-94) and I see an exit marked "Ecorse Road". You'd think that any street marked "Ecorse Road" would lead straight to Ecorse, wouldn't you? Wrong. I dead-ended in Allen Park when it merged with Allen Road!

I loved Ecorse. I taught in the high school, four classes four days a week. I ran weekly dances for the teen-agers and with the profits bought the top songs of the "Hit Parade" to play each week. I was stationed with **Monsignor Tobias Morin**, who was pastor, and **Father Jim DeWitt.** I loved it there, but was destined to only be there one year.

Vacationing In Mexico

I had decided to always take my annual three week vacation in Mexico in order to keep my language skills sharp and to increase in my knowledge of the cultural background of those Latinos I worked with.

Priests usually went on vacation with other priests, sometimes with laymen they knew well. So, in 1958, I went to Mexico were several of my classmates, including Fathers Don Dacey, Emmanuel Lotito and Ted Blaszczyk. The picture below was taken that summer.

Vacationing in Mexico in 1958: Fr. Ted Blaszczyk, Attorney Miguel
Valdez Villarreal and Fr. Emmanuel Lotito (now married) have a
refreshing Pepsi in an Acapulco cantina.

A Note About Muskrat

**You eat muskrat on Fridays during Lent because
it's "seafood"... then you must be a Michigan resident
from "downriver"**

Traditional folklore says that the early French settlers
who were Catholic came across this animal that swam in
the water and wondered if the Church would classify it as
a fish so they could eat it on Fridays. Rome knew no
more about muskrats than people from San Francisco.
So Rome gave permission for people in the "downriver"
area of Michigan to eat muskrat on Fridays.

So, I was told, if you are a Catholic in Ecorse, you have to eat Muskrat. I did three times. The firemen made muskrat dinner for me twice. It was delicious. The parishioners put on a "Muskrat Dinner" on a Friday in Lent. It was terrible. I have not eaten muskrat since.

The Presbyterian Pastor Took Up Our Collection

The **Reverend George Coleman**, who pastored the Presbyterian church across Jefferson Avenue, had been the Minister there before **Mary Lou Price** crossed the street and became a Catholic.

You can imagine her surprise and puzzlement when she was sitting in a pew at our last Mass on Sunday (which started at 12:30 p.m.) and her former pastor sticks a collection basket in front of her!

George told me later that he always wondered what Catholic did at Mass, and that morning his services ended early so he walked across the street to stand in the rear of the crowded church. The ushers were short handed so they asked this nice looking young man to help them. He didn't have time to explain so he accepted the role and helped them out.

Monsignor Tobias ("Toby") Morin

Monsignor Tobias Morin had been in Ecorse just about forever! He was a great guy and almost 90 years old at the time that I was stationed with him. He talked about riding his bicycle from Our Lady of Lourdes parish in River Rouge to the "mission" at Ecorse many years earlier. I asked him one day when he returned from a trip if I could carry his suitcases upstairs for him. He responded, "Young man, I'd never have reached 90 years old if I let people carry my suitcases for me!"

The dear old monsignor was deathly worried about not having enough money to live on in his old age. (Diocesan clergy had a very small pension at that time and were on their own when they retired, although they could live cheaper if some pastor invited them to stay in his parish rectory.) His concern highlighted one of his idiosyncrasies - the lighted candles in the church was his source of personal income! He bought the candles out of his own money – small ten cent variety or the large dollar ones – and then he collected every Sunday morning whatever money came in the coin boxes at each votive stand. Then, he placed the coins in a suitcase and left every Sunday after the last Mass for his sister's home in Toledo where he would count it and bank it. We laughed about it, especially when he encouraged the practice of lighting votive lights in his sermons. We figured the most he every got out of this was under twenty dollars a week!

We bought him a bumper pool table for Christmas. He was good at pool and taught me how to put enough English on the cue ball so that it would curve around a ball to strike a ball behind it. We played almost every night after dinner. I even make a crown from cardboard covered with aluminum foil that the winner had to wear while we played. It delighted the Monsignor to get to wear the crown. I enjoyed seeing the old fellow so happy over such a simple thing.

The "old man" was part of history. He knew the Ecorse folks who had fun making some money rowing back and forth to Canada with liquor during the prohibition days. Most were parishioners. He also recalled when the Chicago boys moved in big time under Al Capone. The fun had ended. Now it was guns and bribery so that the Ecorse police even escorted the trucks to get them early on the road back to Chicago!

Monsignor Morin died at the age of 96. He was still driving his big Mercury until shortly before his death.

Quoting The "Famous" Poet

As I said earlier, I never was a great preacher. So when I was asked to give the main address at the Ecorse Public High School Graduation in 1959, I worked hard in preparing for the talk. The theme was simple. "You are about to set sail in your ship of life – don't let it sink like one of Kaiser shipyards Victory ships sank in 1943 right after it was launched." I wanted a strong ending, kind of sentimental that had a theme of sailing a ship. A poem! That is what was needed! A strong, moving, sentimental poem about sailing a ship!

I went to two libraries. I looked through countless books of poems. Don't sailors write poems? I could not find one poem that was helpful.

So I wrote a poem – strong, sentimental, and meaningful. It fit right in at the end of the talk. Perfect! I introduced it by saying, "And, as that famous poet wrote…"

Like I said, priests never lie, they might exaggerate.

Father Clement Kern Suggested That I Study In Puerto Rico

Father Kern told me that the archdiocese would pay me to spend the summer of 1959 studying Spanish in Ponce, Puerto Rico. It would be in the new language school opened there by the famous Monsignor Ivan Illich. At first I said "No way!" because I loved Ecorse so and knew I already spoke quite acceptable Spanish.

He assured me that I would return to Ecorse after the summer and said I deserved a little "vacation" (what a line!). So I went. I enjoyed it. I liked visiting places local Puerto Ricans had come from – like San Lorenzo, Utuado and other small towns. I even renewed acquaintance with Sister Bernadette, IHM, who had taught me in the seventh grade at Gesu School. But I never returned to Ecorse. At the end of the summer, my next assignment was to be Father Kern's assistant pastor at Most Holy Trinity Church in Detroit!

That is my 1958 Pontiac, purchased with departure donations from Adrian parishioners, parked at my new assignment at St. Francis Xavier Parish in Ecorse, Michigan

Trinity In 1959

You have to picture it. When I arrived at Most Holy Trinity it was bustling and booming. They hadn't started work on the downtown section of the Lodge expressway yet. The Baker streetcar still ran on Porter Street from downtown Detroit and headed straight out Vernor Highway towards Holy Redeemer church. Our condemned old school building was still in constant use. Many Puerto Rican farm workers were still housed in the basement of the school. (Father Kern had saved them when they were stranded.) Apartments near the church were full of crowded families of every nationality. Chinatown was two blocks away. Old Mr. Zerafa ran his shoe repair "kitty-corner" across the street in the basement of one of the apartment buildings. The Mexican restaurant located on Sixth street (at the alley behind the old convent) was still selling baptismal records stolen from our rectory with our seal embossed on them for thirty dollars each. (It helped to prove your citizenship if you were baptized here the day you were born or close to it.)

I loved it. It was all changed quickly during the following two years. The Lodge Expressway came through along with Urban Renewal. They cruelly pushed out the poor, the elderly, and the newcomers. These changes uprooted lives already hurt and destabilized by a thousand big and little influences from unemployment to illness, from language difficulties to --- you name it.

Father Kern – You Had To Love Him

Father Kern. He was the man! Small in stature, big in heart, ideas, and ideals. He was known at "Detroit's Labor Priest" and as the "Saint of Skid Row". Father Clement H. Kern had been pastor of Most Holy Trinity for over ten years. He would continue to be pastor there for almost thirty more years.

"Clem" was how priests knew him. Because his Dad was very active in Pontiac in the labor movement's early days, Clem was always interested, involved with, and supportive of labor unions. When the communists wanted to take over the struggling labor unions in the late thirties and early forties, Clem joined with **Father Raymond Clancy** and **Father Karl Hubbell** to start Labor Schools to teach union members a solid rationale (based on Pope Leo XIII's encyclical), how to organize, how to run a union meeting, how to filibuster in order to keep control of a local union in your hands, and the many concepts of social justice and Cooperativism. Their students formed the A.C.T.U., the Association of Christian Trade Unionists. They even published a newspaper for their organization that continued to instruct members on the highest ideals of labor.

Social Concerns and Efforts of Father Kern

Starting to live and work with Father Kern has to be similar to a position which would combine the roles of the assistants to **Mother Teresa**, **John L. Lewis**, the **Ringling Brothers**, **Pope John XXIII** and a juggling pan-handler.

In the parish house lived the two of us officially assigned there and normally at least eleven other priests. **Monsignor Thomas Jobs** lived in the room next to mine; he was the director of the archdiocesan office of the Propagation of the Faith, concerned with the financial and spiritual support of missionaries. **Father Valentine Rodriguez**, a refugee from Spain's General Franco, taught at Marygrove College and was living with us, until he accepted a position teaching at Acquinas College in Grand Rapids.

For all five years that I was there, Father Kern provided room and board for eight to ten priests who had problems of one sort or another, usually because of the disease of alcoholism. It was a rare day that all of them were sober. Like most victims of that disease, they were wonderful men, good, smart and often too "soft" or sentimental. I liked them and they sure made life interesting. For example, taking a call from a bartender to come get this fellow claiming to be a priest, while he was insulting **Sonny Elliott**, Channel 4's weathercaster. Or, being embarrassed when one, completely naked, entered our Thursday night dinner when we had dignitaries as guests. Or, when **Sister Maura Morrissey, IHM**, the principal of our school, laughingly informed us that the priest with mental illness had just preached heresy to the nuns while he celebrated Mass in the convent. Even with all the incidents, I can truly say that I liked each one of them and my life was enriched by working with them.

The Thursday night dinner was special. That was the night that we had the *free Legal Clinic* and the *free Cabrini Medical Clinic*. All the lawyers and doctors were invited to join us as well as any teachers, social workers, politicians, or dignitaries of any kind. It was a crowded dining room with intriguing conversations. In the hallway outside, on the crowded benches of old church pews, some twenty persons usually were waiting to see Fr. Kern or to talk with a lawyer. Over in the school, another crowd was waiting for the doctors. I wish I could remember all the names of the doctors and lawyers. There were doctors like **Dayton O'Donnell** from Providence Hospital, **Tom Stock** from Mount Carmel Mercy Hospital, and **Mike Brennan** and **Robert Nixon** from Henry Ford Hospital. Lawyers included **Jim O'Hara** (later a congressman), **Michael Talbot** (now a Judge on the Michigan Court of Appeals), **Bill Broderick** (later with the State Department and then with Ford Motor), his brother, **Jim Broderick** (later a Federal Worker's Compensation judge in Washington, DC), **Sander Levin** (now a long time congressman) and **Frank Markey**, who had gone to Gesu grade school with me. I should note that Sandy Levin's wife, **Barbara Levin,** did marvelous work with the children from our grade school!

The *Cabrini Clinic* coordinator was one person who had serious responsibilities, coordinating everything, including maintaining medical treatment files on each person. I can picture the faces of some of those great women, but only remember **Mary Medrano's** name and, of course, **Sr. Mary Ellen Howard, RSM**, who currently has the task. Helping in the clinic to sort and file all the drug samples donated by physicians were the dedicated wives of area pharmacists. On Clinic night, the Alcoholic Anonymous group (largest in Detroit, mainly because of Skid Row fellows) met in the adjoining cafeteria. Those members were welcome to join the long line in the clinic for vitamin shots. I passed through their meeting almost every Thursday just to greet them and make them feel welcome. I worried (for just a short bit) about my "reputation" when I discovered they thought I was a member. But when you live with Father Kern, you just learn to do your work and don't worry about what people think.

There was also a *foot clinic* run every week for over 15 years by a podiatrist, **Dr. Kaplan**. For the fellows on Skid Row, this was a real blessing. They were on their feet more than most people, walking, often in ragged and/or ill-fitting shoes. Dr. Kaplan's work was a real God-send to these men. (I also learned from Fr. Kern, that there were a lot of good-willed "volunteers" who lost their enthusiasm after a month of two; he told me the real gems are the ones who continue doing volunteer work year after year! So a good man like Dr. Kaplan deserves a lot of credit.)

The Dental Hygienists Society of Wayne County operated a *Dental Clinic* where they checked and cleaned the teeth of children in our school. One of these volunteers, who was the daughter of my Dad's friend, **Carl Schoeniger**, was afraid her car might be broken into in our neighborhood. I assured her there would not be any problems, but if she was worried, she could park it on the street right outside my window where I could watch it all day long. Which I did. Faithfully.

When she returned, she discovered that someone had jacked her car up on the far side and removed both of her wheels! I don't know if she ever returned. (I always suspected that someone new in town, probably from the suburbs, had to be responsible for things like that.)

Father Kern had as many as six stores and many trucks and places for alcoholics to work and to live when he started *Corktown Coop*, collecting, repairing and selling used clothing and furniture and other household goods. It was started by an energetic fellow named **Ed** (I can't remember his last name). **Dom Helder Camara**, the saintly archbishop of Recife, Brazil, had started a similar operation for the Skid Row men in Rio de Janeiro which I later visited.

That was when I started making comparisons between these two saints. The beauty of Fr. Kern's approach is that he trusted everyone, giving each person another chance to make it or to fail, and never judging them either way. Dom Helder, however, hired professional social workers to hold the more responsible positions. Both ways are acceptable, I decided. The good side of Fr. Kern's approach is that many fellows (well, *some* men) got themselves together and re-entered what we define as mainstream living. The bad side of that approach is that every so often someone walked off with the treasury. Today, *Corktown Coop* no longer exists. But Dom Helder's program was still going in Rio, the last I heard.

Since he believed that people who have no income other than Social Security could put their funds together to live cheaper, he organized St. Elizabeth's Home for Women, a home for men and a home for married couples. The one for women thrived, especially after moving to a home on Webb Street near Woodrow Wilson Avenue in Detroit. I'm sure it was because the women took turns cleaning and cooking. After being in operation for more than 15 years, the men's program failed probably because the men did not want to do those household jobs and had to pay someone to cook and someone else to clean! The third home failed early. I never knew the reason.

Lou Murphy and his wife ran the Catholic Worker Program in the area. **Dorothy Day**, who founded the movement came through at least once a year and always had lunch with us, because of her close friendship with Father Kern. The Murphy's dedicated their entire lives helping the poor, especially the homeless and maintained a soup kitchen for meals and a farm in Canada to grow food that they would use in their program. They were a family that could be admired by all. One of their daughters, **Sheila Cockrell**, is a member of the Detroit City Council today, carrying on the community dedication of her parents.

As Urban Renewal spread, there were many opportunities to use vacated buildings. Owners of buildings in the area were afraid of losing value should someone vandalize their property before HUD paid them. They didn't want their buildings to stay vacate for too long. One of Fr. Kern's great ideas was to open up three "Reading Rooms" in vacant store fronts on Michigan Avenue. We contacted the owners who were happy to let us use them if we simply paid our own utility usage.

Many of the folks on Skid Row, whatever the reason for being there, were really self conscious of the stares they would get from "ordinary citizens" – stares that would silently say, "What are you doing lying around on MY park bench wearing those rags and looking so dirty!"

The Reading Rooms were places where they could go. They could sit down, be warm, listen to the radio or television, read, have a warm cup of coffee, or even doze off – this was heaven! No one stared at them with haughty and disgusted glares. Fr. Kern insisted that there be current copies of the *Wall Street Journal* at each place. He also asked poets and actors who were in town to recite their poems or read a section from scripture for the men. Neat, eh?

(Father Kern also used a vacated building on Alexandrine near Woodward as a half-way house for prisoners who were three time losers. They couldn't have been released without that house. **Ed Robinson**, a young African-American teacher, volunteered to run that house and stayed with it for 20 years, moving it, changing it to a substance abuse facility, etc. Ed deserves much credit which he never received for his time and dedication!)

When Skid Row moved four years later, I gave a great man the funds to open a Reading Room in the new location on Cass Avenue. He wanted to do some volunteer work for these men. He happened to be homosexual but I had known him and this fact for several years and trusted him as I would trust any heterosexual man. Well, the "Chancery" found out that this priest (meaning me) was sponsoring a homosexual on Skid Row. I was called in by Monsignor "Bud" Kearns who said this was not a good thing. I sure was nervous. I did explain that homosexuals should be allowed to do good things like anyone else. When I left I felt better, so did he. That, however, did not stop me from leaving, nervously anxious to get out of there and actually banging into and then walking through the glass door that separated that wing of the chancery offices!

I was standing, waiting for the elevator, and hearing the secretaries talking excitingly around the corner, saying, "And then, he just walked through the door!"

By the time the elevator finally arrived, I was perspiring.

Open Housing Campaign

I went to many meetings with Fr. Kern and he got me involved with many worth-while causes. For instance, in 1960, a group decided to start an open housing campaign. Three of us were chosen as co-chairpersons, **Abe Citron** and **Mel Ravitz**, both from Wayne State University, and me. I was convinced of the worthiness and justice of the cause. I was not prepared, however, when speaking about the need for such legislation at a state legislative committee hearing in Lansing, to be called a Communist by my fellow Catholics from a Detroit

East Side parish who were there opposing such legislation! I did, however, convince my dad, a prominent local politician, to add his public endorsement in a full page ad in one of the Detroit Newspapers.

The Stranded Puerto Ricans

In 1958, I believe, under an agreement with the Department of Labor of the Commonwealth of Puerto Rico, the sugar beet growers from the Saginaw Valley contracted to bring up 100 selected farm workers from Puerto Rico to work in their fields. These men were carefully screened to make sure they had no drinking problems, police record and anything that would harm the name of this new program. The chartered plane had problems and made an emergency landing in three feet of water off the Carolina shores. The growers association refused any responsibility for these stranded men. Father Kern came to their rescue, brought them to Detroit, housed them in the basement of our school and fed them.

Father Kern also got area employers to hire every one of them, so they had full time jobs at better pay than they would ever have made in the fields. Ford Motor Company was one of the organizations that came through. These men, solid citizens and persons anyone could be proud of, made up the base of what is today's Puerto Rican community in Detroit. They included such outstanding men as **Anastacio Munoz** (and his brothers), **Luis Feliciano** and many others whose names elude me. A very few were still living in the school when I arrived in September of 1959. Father Kern asked me to work with them in a special way for the five years I was there. It was a great honor.

Another Lesson From Father Kern

I thought I had learned too much already from Father Kern until a cold, wintry night when our doorbell rang close to 10:30 p.m. When I opened the door, a man lunged at me with a dagger in his hand. I pushed him back, missing the knife, and had him pinned as tightly as possible as I yelled "Help!" to call Fr. Kern. Clem ran to help me. He saw the knife. He saw the man from Skid Row. He calmly said, in a soft voice, "Peter, I am ashamed of you! What do you think you are doing? Give me that knife and come in and have a cup of hot coffee."

Peter meekly handed the knife to Father Kern. I opened the door and to my utter amazement the two of them walked back to the kitchen for coffee.

I guess I would have called the police. Not Clem. He knew human nature better than most psychiatrists, I believe. It turned out Peter really was anger with Monsignor Jobs and wanted to stab him, not me. I saw Peter occasionally after that night. He was always friendly.

Teaching In The Seminary

Cardinal Dearden decided that Sacred Heart Seminary High School, then known as Cardinal Mooney High School, ought to have some teachers, who were actually doing parish work. It would bring a touch of realism. **Fathers John Echlin**, **Tony Kauffman**, and myself were chosen to be teachers. We were to start in September of 1960. I taught for four years and enjoyed it tremendously. (Teachers have a unique role to play in children's lives as "dreammakers" – what a special profession!) However, since the high school was being accredited, even though we taught "religion", each of us had to take sufficient education courses at the University of Detroit in order that we could be certified as qualified secondary school teachers. That gave me some problems because during the summer of 1960, I was, as usual, living in Monroe

County and working with migrant farm workers. But I was able to do what was required to obtain the credits. My extra efforts included trips to Detroit, required reading, and writing the kinds of papers the professor wanted.

There were some great students, many of which I see from time to time. **Fr. Mike Cooney**, today pastor of St. Peter's Parish in Mount Clemens parish, still accuses me of giving him the only low mark he ever earned in religion! I tried to get my students involved in some of the social work efforts at Most Holy Trinity Church and I do believe having us teaching there did bring a touch of reality to the seminary world.

How We Would Reform The Archdiocese

While the three of us taught in the seminary, one of the thrills we enjoyed was having fun during our one-period break time each day. We conjured up how the three of us would reform the Archdiocese of Detroit. We came up with a list of some twenty ways which we had discussed, argued about, figured on consequences and finalized as good solid suggestions. These ideas included taking the Christmas collection away from the pastors and putting priests on salary so that there would be no jealousy over who got what parish (if all received the same financial rewards). (At the time, they were having some problems getting pastors for poor inner-city parishes. I understand they still do.)

We came up with the idea of having the parish, instead of the priest, receive the stipends offered for Mass intentions, baptisms, and marriages. We even boldly suggested eliminating some parishes, like St. Vincent's and some others. We even thought the archdiocese should start hiring minorities since they did not have even one African-American employed in their offices. I can't recall all of the suggestions. I gave the list to Msgr. Jobs who had lunch in the chancery dining room with all the priest staff and the Cardinal every day. Many of the ideas were implemented. Just a year later, I was asked to select the first Black employee of the Archdiocese and I sent **Walta Belle,** who was hired and worked there, starting in the copy room. She stayed there, I believe, until she retired many years later. I really don't know if all the changes were the result of the ideas from the three of us or not. In any case, since some pastors were slightly disturbed at the loss of income, I never publicly acknowledged having said anything about Christmas collections or stipends until this writing!

"I've Got A Mother, Too!"

Every parish gets phone calls regularly asking if we know anyone looking for a good place to live in return for taking care of their aging parent. Of course, these callers really want to avoid paying any decent salary, if any. We often got more than our share of these calls at Most Holy Trinity. One day shortly after Christmas one year, a nice woman called and said she needed a "live-in" to help her take care of her two bed-ridden parents. When I asked Fr. Kern, he suggested **Sally Jo** who came to church frequently, needed work and lived just a block away in a boarding house on Fourth Street, corner of Porter. I went over, and found Sally Jo who was happy to have a job. The woman would even pay her! I called the woman who came and got Sally Jo, suitcase and all, and took her to their home off Livernois near Grand River..

It was almost three weeks later that a call came in from this woman. It was a very cold January day. She was shaking, she said, as she told me that she returned home from work to find that Sally Jo was gone and so were both of her bed-ridden parents!

Like it was my fault.

I told her I would do what I could to find out where Sally Jo was. I had to drive around because they had not yet constructed the pedestrian bridge over the not-yet opened expressway. I knocked on the padlocked door of her old apartment. As expected there was no response. I knocked at the manager's door. He said he hadn't seen Sally Jo, but her best friend was in Apartment 6 which apartment had to be entered from the side street. It was upstairs and to the right. As I ascended the rickety stairs, I could already hear the loud talking and the music coming from Apartment 6. I knocked on the door and when it was opened by a drunken, naked woman, I could see a dark room with little light and about twelve barely dressed middle-aged persons, mostly drunk. But what immediately caught my eye was a very elderly woman propped up in a chair on the far side of the room, bundled in a blanket and trembling with a mixture of fear, illness and cold. The woman who answered the door immediately said, "Oh, you must be looking for Sally Jo's woman. Let me help you. I've got a mother, too!"

The lady at the door put on a wrap and I carried the elderly lady to my car wrapping her in another blanket. Sally Jo came running after me explaining she just needed a drink and had left the man with a neighbor and brought the woman on the bus with her because "she was too sick to leave her alone".

I don't think I ever again sent a stranger to help take care of someone's aged parents.

(I take that back. Later on I did send a woman to help in my sister, Polly Denton's home as a "live in". Polly and I laughed when she explained that she wondered where all her food was disappearing to. It took almost four months before she discovered the woman had snuck her sister in and Polly was actually supporting the two of them!)

The Fiftieth

Dad was so proud of the fact that they were to be married fifty years. He designed his own invitation with hand drawings of their life together. We had a wonderful celebration starting with a Mass with Cardinal Dearden present at the Convent of the Sacred Heart in Bloomfield Hills, Michigan on June 21, 1961.

It meant so much to Dad that from that day on, whenever he read of some couple celebrating the fiftieth wedding anniversary, he sent them a congratulatory note even though he usually did not even know them personally.

What was special about that day to me was that it was the second time in our lives that all of the eleven children were together. (Dolores was in a semi-cloistered order when she entered the convent before Danny was even born.) The next time we were all together was just fourteen months later at Dad's funeral.

Another Knock On The Door

The Urban Renewal project was across the street from us. They had vacated all the apartments and dwellings and the buildings stood as barren reminders of delayed hopes and lost memories. When I would go for an evening stroll, however, they were almost frightening, since I knew that there were always men from Skid Row asleep in those windowless rooms.

Charlie Hurst told me that he was asleep in one building on Abbott after he and a friend shared a bottle of cheap wine. He said he woke up when the building shook and he thought, "It's an earthquake!" He said he ran to the window just in time to see a crane swinging a huge iron ball against the brick building! "BANG!!!" Charlie said he woke his friend and they scurried out of that place faster than rabbits.

This leads me to tell you what happened to me one evening in 1962. Earlier, that afternoon, when I returned from teaching at the seminary, a man approached me and asked where he could wash his hands. I showed him the nearby spigot and went in the house. It turned out that he was responsible for what I am about to tell you. He was using our spigot to wash blood off of his hands and shirt.

That spring evening was a warm night. We finished talking to people who had come for this or that, so it was after nine o'clock. I heard a knocking at the front door. Unusual. They could have rang the doorbell. I opened the door to find a man I knew from Skid Row who was bleeding all over. He had been stabbed many times in a room on the fourth floor of the abandoned apartment. He explained that his pal had also been stabbed and might even be dead but that I should call the police and go over there at once.

You understand, dear reader, that I am normally a brave and courageous man. At least that's how it is in my dreams. But on this dark night, even armed with a flashlight, to enter the abandoned building where a murderer might be waiting, made me slightly hesitant. I asked Monsignor Jobs to go with me. (I had already called the police.) Monsignor Jobs agreed to wait at the bottom of the stairs. I was too slow as I climbed because I had just passed the second floor when I heard several policemen coming up behind me and telling me to "get the "h" out of here, Father!"

I was always law-abiding. So I did.

The man left in the room was dead. He and his friend had cashed a Social Security check to buy wine and someone saw they had money and followed them.

It was a shock to me when the police started accusing the bleeding man of killing his friend and a sergeant actually beat him up when he should have been in the hospital! The Detroit Police now have a more humane approach than some officers did in those years. The police did, however, find the murderer and bring him to trail.

The Spanish-Speaking Priests: Club Of Our Own

The number of priests in the Archdiocese who could speak Spanish was limited. **Fathers Clement Kern, Bill Kearns, Bill Carolin, Jim Sheehan, Joe Melton, Jerry Fraser, John DeWitt, Bill Brennan**, a Basilian priest from St. Anne de Detroit, and a Redemptorist priest from Holy Redeemer and me. Not many. Under Father Kern's leadership we met almost every month to exchange ideas and motivate ourselves. It was a "club of our own" and we moved from parish to parish taking one another's places. It helped. We were able to learn from one another and to support one another's efforts..

Human Relations Office

One day, true to form (Fr. Kern was always coming up with ideas) Father Kern asked what I thought about getting all the diocesan priests together who were interested in helping the African-American community and having lunch at Most Holy Trinity. We could even invite the newly appointed **Archbishop (but not yet Cardinal) Dearden**. Great idea. We made up a list of all the priests we knew. We got on the archbishop's schedule and I was given the task to call and invite everyone. It was only then that Clem said we need to ask the Archbishop for something. It turned out that we would suggest that he establish a Human Relations Department to work with African-Americans and with the Spanish-Speaking population. Clem announced this at the luncheon, in his own inimitable way, slightly exaggerating, when stating that "We have all talked about and agreed that it is vital to this archdiocese that a Human Relations office or department be established as soon as possible." (This was really a surprise to almost every priest there, not just the archbishop!)

And it happened fast. **Father Maiberger** was appointed to be the first director, and he was followed by **Father James J. Sheehan** (when Fr. Maiberger was discovered to be terminally ill). Wonderful works were accomplished through that office.

The Cursillo

I'm not sure what year it was, probably 1962 or 1963. Three men from St. Michael's Parish in Southfield came to chat with Father Kern about a new kind of spiritual retreat centered on your relationship with Christ. It was an import from Spain and was called the "Cursillo de Cristiandad" or, in English, "The Little Course in Christianity". For short, most people just call it the "Cursillo" (pronounced "ker-see-yo").

They were from a parish staffed by Franciscan priests and had attended, with a large number of others, the Cursillo in Cincinnati, which, coincidently, was under the direction of the Franciscan friars there. They wanted to invite the "Team" from Cincinnati to come to Detroit and start the movement here. Father Kern listened carefully and said he was interested and would get back to them.

Dear reader: you must understand that there is a bond of love among all Christians. However, under this umbrella of love, there is sometimes a trifle of jealousy between diocesan priests and priests who are members of religious orders. For Clem to have the Franciscans come here and run a movement was like President Bush asking the Democrats to run the Republican National Convention (or vice versa).

The plot thickens. "George", he says to me, "Why don't you go up to Saginaw where Fr. Bob Keller has the Cursillo going in Spanish? You make the retreat there, learn all you can and maybe we can work things out to get it going here on our terms".

So I did, and then we did.

We had two Cursillos in Spanish, one put on by the team from Saginaw, the other by a team from Lorainne, Ohio. Together our "club" of Spanish-speaking priests got the best Hispanic laymen from Adrian, Detroit, Pontiac, Ecorse, Erie, Imlay City, and Port Huron involved. Then we held two in English, one using the Franciscan-trained team from Cincinnati and the other using Fr. Bob Keller's newly formed English-speaking team from Saginaw.

All of this time, we were selecting and training our own teams to run them here (under the guidance of a diocesan priest – Father Jim Sheehan, whom Clem "conned" into believing it was under his department). Jim, shortly after, organized Cursillos for women, both in English and in Spanish.

It was a rewarding experience, but I sure was happy that someone else was running it.

Sr. Rita Mary And The Best Mexican Music In Town

Most of the parishes where I conducted services in Spanish for the migrants gave me the fullest cooperation. When we needed Spanish hymns, I would give the sheet music to the organist and thus we had music the Spanish-speaking migrants would feel at home with. Only in the parish where I lived during several summers did the organist object, indicating some resentment at having to do anything special for 'those" people. So an eighth grade girl who could play the piano came to my rescue at St. Anthony's parish near Temperance, Michigan. Her name was **Rita Mary Olszewsk**i. I gave her the Spanish sheet music and she used her free time to practice them on the church organ.

I don't remember how many summers Rita Mary played for the migrant services. I do remember purchasing the sheet music for her when I was in Mexico City the following winter, so that during the second summer she played, we must have had the very best Mexican Music every played (up to then) in any Catholic church in the six counties of the archdiocese!

While I was off doing other things, Rita Mary entered the convent and became a Religious Sister of Mercy. Subsequently, she taught my daughter, Karon, in the eighth grade at Shrine Grade School in Royal Oak, and stayed a constant advocate for the poor and for social justice. Today, **Sr. Rita Mary Olszewski, RSM**, serves as a valuable aide to **Bishop Thomas Gumbleton**, the wonderful, activist Auxiliary Bishop of Detroit. She belongs to *Pax Christi* (a group working for world peace) and is very involved in all peace issues.

In Praise Of The Teamsters

The teamsters originally were the strong men who drove the teams of horses that pulled the wagons filled with lumber and other cartage. Historically, in Detroit, these wagon drivers for the lumber industry organized for their own protection and eventually had a real battle against thugs hired by the lumber industry until their union was recognized. That is the history that I have been told.

In any case, driving wagons, and now, driving trucks, demands skills but not a college education. It used to be the kind of job you could get if you knew a minimal amount of English. You didn't have to be "connected", but it did help if you had a friend and needed a job to support yourself and your family. Often brawny, the teamsters got a reputation as rough and ready men.

So what, I say. I found the Teamsters to be uniquely sympathetic to the poor and downtrodden. I could add that while I found so many old men living lonely lives in boarding houses in the center of the city, those who had retirement checks from having been Teamster members, were able to live better that any of the others. Jimmy Hoffa helped get that for "his boys".

More than that, when some of these old men and less often, old women, needed to supply blood donors in order to have an operation (which was needed in those days) only the Teamsters and the University of Detroit would release it from their blood banks. Other organizations would turn their requests down saying, "He has to be a member" or "He must replace it within four weeks". A simple call to **Bobby Holmes**, at Teamster headquarters on Trumbull Avenue, got the blood needed for these people who had no relatives or friends to turn to.

When we discovered that men who wanted to work and could only get jobs as "bill passers" had to wait in lines from 3 or 4 a.m. to be chosen to go on the trucks, we tried several unions to find someone who would organize them. The men were taken advantage of so much. Even the truck driver got to select his crew and would always pick his favorites. These were often men who would give him a small kick-back from their meager pay. The Teamsters came through to organize them. I made up some flyers and passed them around the neighborhood and with the Skid Row men. (Many bill passers are not homeless, just poor persons living in boarding houses or low priced apartments.) Over 200 men showed up for the union's organizational meeting in our school cafeteria in the spring of 1964. Almost every company agreed to a contract that increased the pay and spelled out a fair method of worker selection. It is my understanding that the union no longer exists. Every time I see men going door to door, I look down at their worn shoes and ragged clothes and wonder how they are treated today...

Jimmy Hoffa and **Bert Brennan** decided to help our parish when we had to raise money to build the new school. Bert was a co-chair of a fund raiser. **Ed Levy, Sr.**, who ran a stone and gravel company on Dix Highway near Dearborn, served as the other co-chair. Fox Movies allowed us to use a premier of their new movie "*The Story of Ruth*" as the fund raiser. It turned out to be a lousy movie. However, the Teamsters alone brought in over $27,000 in ticket sales. **Ed Levy** chipped in and had me get some money out of his friend, **Max Fisher**. (He told me to exaggerate his gift and ask Max to give that same amount. Max gave half, which turned out to be more than Ed's gift! – Priests don't lie, of course, but they will go along with exaggeration.)

How To Motivate

Father Kern was convinced that you continually had to keep before the minds of all parish works the spiritual rationale for their efforts.

For this reason he held an "*evening of recollection*" every month to which everyone working in the parish was invited, from the nuns to the members of parish organizations, from the coop homes to the doctors and lawyers, in short, everyone.

To me, it was a beautiful means of motivation, of using the "mystique", the power of our Faith, that Dom Helder Camara, saintly Archbishop of Recife, often talked about.

Vic Venegas

Father Kern paid the way through high school of many kids in the area. **Vic Venegas** was one of them. He attended Assumption High School, across the bridge in Windsor. Vic's Dad, **Moises**, ran a gas station and garage for car repair on Vernor Highway at the corner of Fourth Street. They lived on the first floor of an apartment building next door. Vic's Mother, **Mary Venegas**, was a great help in the parish and had a delightful sense of humor. Vic had a sister we called "**Cuddy**" and a younger brother, **Paul Venegas**. I could speak highly of each one of them, but here I really just want you to know about Vic.

Vic Venegas came to me while he was in high school and offered to volunteer to coach athletics to our grade school students. Vic became the permanent coach – I have no idea for how many years. The parish and those kids will always be indebted to him.

Joe Hartman was the new Personnel Director for the Wayne County Road Commission, succeeding **John McElroy** who retired. **Bettye Misuraca**, who, like Vic, became a lifelong friend of mine, worked for both of them. But it was Joe Hartman who promised me that he would give jobs to two people that I would send to him every spring. If they worked out well, mowing along the expressways, he would keep them as permanent employees. I sent Vic Venegas and "Big Red" (I knew him as a member of the Stiletto Gang when I worked with them – that's another story). Big Red didn't last. Vic, however, remained as a Road Commission employee until he retired.

Vic has been close to me ever since. I see him still on a regular basis since we both are members of the Board of Directors the **Father Clement H. Kern Foundation. The Kern Foundation** was begun for the purposes of raising funds to assist the poor and for promoting social justice which Clem supported.

The Stiletto Gang

I was too innocent. So, when "Big Louie", a hefty seemingly friendly Latino wanted me to meet some of the *Stiletto Gang* which boasted of some 150 members in the area, I hopped in his car. It was 9 or 10 at night on a hot summer evening when we drove into an alley behind Vermont Street. South of Michigan Avenue. Our headlights caught some 12 or so youths scattering in every direction. When Louie flicked his headlights onto "bright" and back, the youths calmly returned to await his car's arrival. A garage with its entrance off the alley was their meeting place.

From that day on for several weeks, I had a lot of contact with Louie and the gang members. Until one day, an officer of the Youth Division of the Police Department met with Father Kern and I. He told us of some of the things that they suspected Luis and the top officers were involved in. Such as drugs, some violence, and especially getting Hispanic girls pregnant so they would be thrown out of their homes and then the gang would give them housing in return for the girls pushing drugs and serving as prostitutes. I don't know if any of these accusations were true. But I did shy away from much further contact.

The Fellows On Skid Row

I'm sure you have had the same kind of experiences I have had. You see a person and perhaps make some observation, even a judgment, but you never really know that person. But if you have a chance to talk with that same person, hear his or her life story, find out his or her worries and concerns, know about his or her aches and pains, and, in my case especially, hear that person's sins and desires to be better – well, now you see that individual in a different light, as a real person. Usually you start to like that person when you really know him or her. He or she becomes a "friend".

The same is true about the fellows I came to know who lived on Skid Row.

I got to know a man who lived a miserable life but had a son in Philadelphia who was a priest. The son had me look in on his dad once in a while. I was talking to him once while he lay on his cot in a flophouse dormitory when a man came up and broke an empty wine bottle on his head. He continued the conversation as if nothing had happened without even brushing the glass off of his undershirt.

There was a "blind" "veteran" who wore his veteran's cap proudly with dark glasses on his eyes and a tin cup in his hand as he begged on Michigan Avenue near Griswold. I used to know him by name. Needless to say he was neither blind nor a veteran and I could only tease him about it when no one could see or hear us. But sometimes when I walked downtown, I would hear a "Hi Father!" when no one was around and I was still thirty feet away!

Speaking of blindness, I got to know a very nice man in the area named George. Out of the blue, someone came to tell me that George was home from the hospital and was now blind. It seems he had drunk a large quantity of pure alcohol and it was so hard on his system that he went blind. From that point on, I brought him Holy Communion every first Friday of the month at a one room apartment on 4th Street. When he got a Seeing Eye dog, he started to get out some. He was just another casualty of alcoholism.

"Singing Sam" was a nice, very intelligent man who was a librarian. His lived on the Avenue whenever he was drunk. Many of those who lived on the streets would get themselves arrested when it got too cold by throwing a brick through a store's window while a police officer was nearby. Then they could get a ninety day sentence for being "Drunk and Disorderly" or whatever charge so they could spend the winter months in a warm place like the Detroit House of Correction (which everyone called "Dehoco"). Singing Sam was different. He was the librarian at Dehoco. They needed him. When his ninety days were up, a police car would bring him directly to our rectory. The officers would put his two suitcases under our back porch and Sam would go on a four or five day binge. During those days, he would sing as long and as loud as he could on the bridge across the Lodge expressway (and next to my bedroom window). When the time was up, he would be picked up by the police, taken to court with his suitcases, get a ninety day sentence and go back to work as the librarian.

I had started a *Legion of Mary* group with the fellows on Skid Row. We meet weekly in one of the "Reading Rooms". The assignment was always to ask them to rescue anyone who was ill or freezing in an alley and I would take them to Receiving Hospital. **Henry Pierce** was an orderly in the Emergency Room and he helped get them hospitalized. Hospitals, at that time, didn't accept alcoholism as an illness, but if you said that this man had "DTs" ("Delirium Tremens") he would be admitted! Henry sure saved many lives by using that phrase.

But some would die. In the hospital or in an alley. Clem thought that every person deserved a decent burial. We would get the word off the street that Bill Jones (or whatever name was used) had died. Clem would send me to the morgue to claim the body.

Clayton Brundage Sr., the saintly undertaker, would bury the person with whatever money we could get from welfare or Social Security. The Archdiocese was very cooperative, each time allowing a free burial in Holy Sepulcher Cemetery. Most of them we really did not know, and especially didn't know if they were Catholic. But they did have a decent burial. Clem would send me to the morgue and I would tell them that I came to claim Bill Jones' body (or whatever name we had been told). They would show me a body and ask if this was Bill Jones. I would say, "Yes, the poor soul!" (It was a good thing they didn't show me more than one and asked which one was Bill Jones!!)

Clem would find a use for a fellow on the Avenue and make a deal with him. The parish would pay for his rent (some nearby rooms went for seven or ten dollars a week), they could eat in the rectory kitchen, plus some pocket money for cigarettes. At times we had six or seven men helping us out under such an agreement. One ran the Job Office, another kept up our records, another did secretarial work, etc. Every so often Clem would tell me to go sober up so-and-so with two quarts of milk "because I need him here right now". Once I had to get a man out of one fellow's bed, another time I had to make a prostitute get off of one of our workers. She dressed real fast and ran off only to return while he drank his milk, saying, "I forgot my belt". Another time I had to convince one of our helpers who was high, to return to his room and quit running around the boarding house naked!

We all survived. I now know there were a lot of things they did not teach us in the seminary.

Monsignor Jobs knew the fellows on Skid Row the best and passed out a roll of quarters, one each, for the men each night. That's what it cost for a bed in one of the flop houses.

Several of the fellows made it off of the Avenue (a nickname for Skid Row at that time, since it was located on Michigan Avenue) and back into jobs and "normal" living. I won't tell much about them so as not to embarrass any relatives.

Flop Houses Made Money

It was at a public hearing sponsored by the Mayor's Committee on Skid Row, I believe, that an owner of one of the flop houses maintained that he had a hard time financially and couldn't provide clean sheets, some personal privacy and other improvements since the men only paid him twenty-five cents each night.

At that point, a builder of high class apartments rose up. He explained that he had to provide a fancy entrance way, parking facilities, a well provided lobby and beautiful landscaping. He said his apartments needed extra cupboards, large rooms, the best heating, air conditioning, stove, refrigerators and washers and dryers for laundry.

He said that while the Flop House owners had very little of these costs, they used only 25 square feet each night for the cot and locker for each man. That came to about $1 for each 100 square feet each night. Some of the flop houses had 200 men each night making fifty dollars nightly. In a month a flophouse made $1,500. At that time, the going price for a 2,000 square foot luxury apartment with all the trimmings was less than one third of that. For this, the owner of the luxury apartments made only eighty-two cents a month per square foot!

The Jesuits Had To Experience The Flop Houses

I will always have the greatest admiration for the members of the Society of Jesus, commonly referred to as *Jesuits*.

In the Novitiate training for young men to become members of the Jesuit religious order, they need to spend one year "in the world", preferably begging or at least living a year of special detachment and poverty. Some wonderful young men were sent, as Jesuit novices, to live with us at Most Holy Trinity for a month.

Father Kern had these young, innocent, mostly middle class-bred young men experience everything in terms of the social ministry of the parish. But he thought the best thing for them would be to walk the streets of Skid Row and spend at least three nights in a flop house. To do this they couldn't shave, could not wear glasses (you'd look like you went to school!), and had to have dirty, unshaven faces and old, dirty and badly-fitting clothes.

When they paid their quarter to enter the flop house, they were entitled to a bed, with a 1-1/2 inch mattress. It had a clean sheet once a week no matter how many people slept on it. They had to get de-loused in a shower. They were encouraged to sleep with their shoes on; otherwise they might wake up and find no shoes to wear. Some of their room mates might show indications of recent drinking, occasionally there would be shouting, but no matter when you got to sleep, a good group got up at four a.m. to go look for work as bill-passers. Everyone had to be out of there by seven.

They did it. And they loved it. But most of them soon dropped out of the Novitiate. I don't think it was because of us or because of Skid Row. But the saintly Director of Novices, **Father Bernard Wernert, SJ,** was given another assignment. Was it because he didn't motivate them to stay? In any case, no novices were ever sent to stay with Father Kern after Father Wernert was reassigned.

Bill Brodhead was one of the novices that dropped out. He went on to become a dedicated family man who also had a commitment to help those in need, He became a United States Congressman, served for a long time on the board of the **Skillman Foundation** and has a very successful law practice.

The 2:30 A.M. Mass On Holy Days –

Long before evening Masses were common in the Catholic parishes, Father Kern had started a 2:30 a.m. *Printers Mass* which we celebrated every Sunday. His reason for getting permission for Mass at that early hour was because the three daily newspapers – the Detroit Times, the Detroit News and the Detroit Free Press –

were all within walking distance of the church and their printing presses finished running the last Sunday papers shortly after 2 a.m. A good crowd of printers showed up for those masses every Sunday. I might also note that the bars had to stop serving drinks at 2 a.m. and, for some reason, we had an even larger number of their customers who made their way to our church, some more directly than others.

Holy Days in the Catholic Church Calendar were special days that were labeled "of Obligation" because of the significance of the feast celebrated. Father Kern insisted that our Mass schedule on Holy Days be the same as on Sundays so as not to confuse people.

On some Holy Days (like the feast of the Immaculate Conception on December 8th) we had almost no one in church. The only exception, each year, was in the early hours of the Feast of Ascension Thursday.

It was on that feast, each year, that the crowd was different. In Catholic high schools throughout the metropolitan Detroit area, the nuns encouraged their students to hold their high school "senior proms" on the Wednesday evening before Ascension Thursday. They also encouraged their students to end the evening's social by attending Mass at our church at 2:30 a.m.

In 1962, **Father Grace Agius, CSB**, the priest who helped out at our parish was the celebrant of that Mass. (We needed him since he could also speak Maltese) My role was to hear confessions until the time to help out in the distribution of the Eucharist. Then I could return to the rectory before him and get back to sleep.

The church was packed with about 1,000 young high school students – seniors and their dates. They were all dressed in formals, the boys with the white-coats of summer tuxedos, the girls with long formal dresses of a whole rainbow of colors, each girl sporting her own corsage of carnations or an orchid. They looked wonderful.

After I helped distribute Communion, I went to the rectory next door and was getting a "midnight snack" when the doorbell rang. I answered it. It was a fellow from Skid Row who asked for Father Kern. I told him, "It's 3:30 a.m.! Father Kern is in bed". The man smiled a gracious smile and simply said, "I just wanted him to know that was <u>the biggest wedding</u> I have ever seen!"

People I Loved At Trinity

I have to mention some names even though I will omit some great ones. But the names I do recall added a richness of their own to my experiences at Most Holy Trinity. **Julia Scott** was our cook for most of the five years. **Rosaura**, direct from Chihuahua, Mexico was the housekeeper. **Joe O'Brien**, a relative of two Jesuit Father O'Briens, answered the door and telephone. **Clem Burke**, who was an elevator expert for Otis, helped us out every week and later married Rosaura and went with her back to Mexico. (A great mystery because he spoke no Spanish, and Rosaura spoke no English!).

John McCarthy was a dedicated retiree who ran our Employment Services. **Jim Gibson** and **Charles Hurst** were volunteers who gave endlessly of their time. **Mary Louise Belle** was a favorite of mine. Her family had me visit her a few years ago just before she died. They still have my wooden statue of the Black Madonna of Montserrat which I gave to their mother.

Lucy Zarate ran the "*Friends of the Family*" which did a lot of home visiting to help women in the parish. Lucy worked hand in hand with the **first Mrs. Henry Ford II** who helped in home visiting. I recall the two of them were making calls and stopped at the Gatt home (a Maltese family) behind Casa Maria. It was so cold that **Mrs. Gatt** gave them each a shot of whiskey to warm them up! Lucy's sister, **Carmen Cortina**, trained youngsters to dance typical Mexican dances. Carmen was special and helped hundreds of children appreciate their great heritage. She and her sister helped me years later when I ran for election in Detroit so that I came in first in several precincts in Southwest Detroit. (I lost the election, however – with enough votes that I could have been mayor of Toledo!).

Sister Maura Morrissey, IHM, was the principal of the grade school and superior of the fine group of religious women. She would whisper special instructions to me, before I spoke to the sisters, such as "Ask **Sr. Casimira (Virginia Parker)** to plan the liturgy for that day" or "Ask **Sr. Agnes Cecile (Ann Currier)** to have her kindergarten children sing". (I forgot the names those sisters used in those days!). The women who worked in the kitchen were a wonderful group and I wish I could remember all their names: they included **Mrs. Frank Azzopardi, Flora, Mrs. Gonzalez** and several others. Many of the same women still help out there. **The ushers** and **Tony Muscat**, our maintenance man, were also special.

Dad Gets Sick And Dies

In the summer of 1962, my Dad died. I was living at St. Anthony's Church near Temperance while I worked with the migrant farm workers. On Sundays, I said two Masses in Erie's St. Joseph Church. Dad had suffered an attack of appendicitis and was recovering from his operation. I had visited him on Friday and saw he was doing well. As I prepared for my first Mass, I received word that he had taken a turn for the worse. I offered that Mass for him.

When I finished Mass, the pastor agreed to preside at the next Mass in my place. Instead there was a call saying

Dad had died. So I stayed and celebrated the second Mass for the peaceful repose of his soul.

Thank God for our Faith. I knew that Dad was in heaven; he was so good. I knew our consciousness of self which is the main part of our soul, is very dependent on our body in this life, during periods of sleep and unconsciousness. But, once death has taken place we are wide awake and conscious of where we are and who we are as we face our God. To be happy in heaven, anything our little minds are capable of wondering about would be known. So Dad would be up there, smiling, knowing all about what was happening with his family here on earth. A great consolation.

The first issues of the Detroit newspapers carried his death in their headlines. Unfortunately, Marilyn Monroe, a sexy movie starl died that same August day. As a result, news of Dad's death moved to the second page.

Mom was fussy about Dad's funeral. She wanted a riderless horse with the boots turned backward, since Dad's first love had been when he served in the Cavalry. The friends of Dad from the veterans organizations, the Knights of Columbus, the Alhambra, the police and firemen, took over the funeral arrangements.

Inspector Vincent Mann, from the Detroit Police Department, and **Charlie Oakman**, then head of the City County Building, coordinated so that Dad's body would lie in state in the City County Building and there would be a funeral procession for two miles from the Ted Sullivan funeral Home to Gesu, with the Detroit Police Band playing funeral dirges with the "boom", pause, "boom" of the base drum striking every other step. It seemed so sad. There were so many veterans present. Six Army generals carried his coffin.

I asked Father Clement Kern to preach at Dad's funeral. He spoke beautifully with the thesis that Dad proved you can be an upstanding, honest and moral person with the highest of ideals and last many years in politics without losing your ideals. (Dad had been elected over and over to serve the people of Detroit for thirty-two years.)

The whole family, all the eleven children gathered for his funeral. We all stayed at the same motel. We would miss him. He was special. Still, we knew he was in heaven, already enjoying what we are still waiting for. It's like knowing that he's won the million dollar lotto! Even though it's still a few years off for us, I'm sure counting on "winning" it myself. Aren't you?

Being so confident of Dad's happiness, we could console Mom best by sharing our joy with her. All eleven of us, with Mom, stayed up late the night before the funeral telling happy and funny stories about life with Dad. So much so, the motel manager called us at 2 a.m. to ask that we "keep it down".

The Dominican Republic

Father Joe Melton (one of the Spanish-speaking priests) had a brother who was in the travel business. This brother had made the retreat called the *Cursillo* and was a strong supporter of Father Kern. He had arranged for Clem to be a chaplain on a cruise ship for postmasters (and their spouses) from around the country. It would be a free trip for Clem who deserved a break and usually had no money.

The ship stopped at the Dominican Republic and Clem, as usual, met up with the local priests and spent the day with them. The day included attending a meeting of the diocesan priests from the city of Santo Domingo. They were talking about their upcoming presidential election at which time a socialist by the name of Juan Bosch was running for election as president. All the priests were talking against Bosch as a "Communist".

You'd have to know Clem. He hated for people to be "run down" and not be able to defend themselves. He also knew that there is a world of difference between a Communist and a socialist. Father Kern, then, in his quiet manner of "dropping bombs" mentioned to the group of priests that he had heard "from the Jesuits" that Juan Bosch was a wonderful Catholic who attended daily Mass and Communion. Well, it had it's intended effect. The priests immediately decided that Juan Bosch had to be a good guy!

Like I said earlier, priests never lie. Some, however, do exaggerate.

The Catechetical Expert

Father Kern's stop in the Dominican Republic somehow had "fallout" for me.

Father Kern told me they needed an "expert" on teaching our faith to people who were illiterate. I had some experience adapting, in my work with migrant farm workers, the catechism that the Chicago priests had written called "La Familia de Dios" ("The Family of God"). I didn't think of myself as an expert. Father Kern, however, possibly exaggerated my talent in speaking to **Monsignor George Higgins** from the Social Action office of the National Catholic Welfare Conference in Washington.

So, I went to the Dominican Republic, where I stayed at the parish of Santa Ana in the capitol. I walked all over the parish area and studied their methodology and approaches to teaching. I visited the headquarters of the country's Cursillo Movement in downtown Santo Domingo, where I sadly noted that the movement was controlled by the wealthy. I wrote out my ideas and recommendations and presented them to an audience of catechetical teachers. These included 1) using the Cursillo movement to train lay leaders; 2) working specifically with married couples (adults, rather than such complete emphasis on children) and 3) using a didactic technique that was deductive based on real life experiences. This latter approach seemed to always have a more lasting effect. I used these three ideas a year later in Brazil.

I thought I was done. No, I was invited to have lunch with the Papal Nuncio, a professional diplomat representing the Vatican in Puerto Rico, the Dominican Republic and Haiti. He asked me to stay and become pastor of one of the many priestless parishes in the country.

Historically, Spain had provided priests and supported them financially for parishes in those countries that were part of the Spanish empire. In 1898, after the Spanish-American War, the priests in Puerto Rico, the Dominican Republic and Cuba were all recalled to Spain. Many parishes in the Dominican Republic remained without pastors when I was there in 1962 and 1963.

Aware of this history, and sympathetic to the need, I told the Papal Nuncio (who was an Archbishop) that while I didn't think I was able to commit myself for a lifetime right now, I knew a lot of priests who spoke Spanish and I could arrange for them to come down during their vacations which could overlap. Perhaps one or more of them might get interested enough to stay. Could he arrange for us to be in charge of a priestless parish for six months? Perhaps in the diocese of Higuey, since I already knew the bishop there. (Bishop Pepin had fled for fear of being assassinated during the worst years of General Trujillo's dictatorship; for a few months he stayed with us at Holy Trinity.) The Nuncio agreed. We would go to the diocese of Higuey, to the city of San Rafael de Yuma.

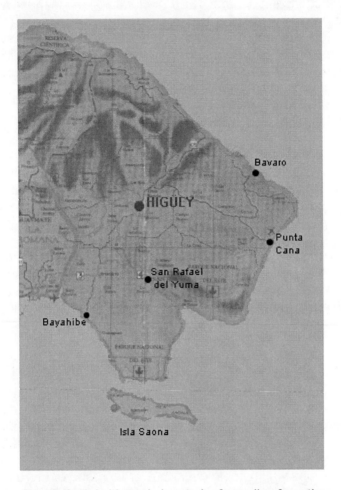

San Rafael de Yuma is located a few miles from the Caribbean on the eastern end of the Dominican Republic

Bring A Tennis Racquet: San Rafael De Yuma

I decided the best approach was to provide a basis of continuity during the six months we would take over a parish. Bishop Pepin agreed that the parish would be San Rafael de Yuma.

I talked to members of my Young Christian Workers group to see who would give six months of their life to help out in that parish. Young people are always so willing to do things for others, once given the opportunity. Vic Venegas, Tom Gonzalez, and Henrieta Limas agreed to go. They would help with catechetics and with youth programs. Then I got someone from Adrian who knew how to start a credit union.

Next: how to get priests. I asked them to spend at least two weeks out of their three week vacations working in a parish in the Dominican Republic. From our local group Jim Sheehan and a couple of others signed up as well as myself. I wrote to some of the Brooklyn and New York City priests that had gone to school with me in Puerto Rico. (I made the mistake of "exaggerating" its benefits, saying that they would "love the tennis courts". Two of them brought their tennis racquets and never spoke to me again!) A good group from the East Coast signed up. I also got a priest from Toledo to go.

It worked out well. We got around on horseback to the smaller towns and baptized and married wherever we went. I remember going to a town on the "other side of the mountain". I had sent word we would be there. The parish church was a solid building, even though it stood empty from 1898 to that day in 1963 when I came riding into town. I must have had 30 weddings to celebrate so they could say they were "married by the priest" and 80 baptisms, with just a few First Communions. Mass, however, was something else. There were firecrackers, huge unruly crowds coming in and out of the church while I tried to celebrate Mass in Latin (which they didn't understand and most had never heard – too bad the "vernacular was just a year away!). It dawned on me – most of them had never been to Mass and didn't know what it was all about! It was like a circus had come to town! They could have sold popcorn.

Now I knew the value of exchange of information, especially in religion.

We had always been trained not to talk when carrying Holy Communion on our person. We were also told never to accept gifts in exchange for the sacraments. So much for the ideal; now for the practical!

While taking Communion on horseback up and down hills, trying to follow the lad on the horse ahead of me (a faster horse, a better rider), from time to time I had to yell at him. Yes, yelling is talking! Then when I gave Communion to a poor, elderly lady, she tied two live chickens by their feet to the post of my saddle and later another old man handed me a dozen eggs to hold in my left hand while I guide the horse down slippery slopes. Well, you guess it, so much for not accepting gifts. I decided, I'd rather break the rule than hurt those great folks' feelings.

A mother approached me in San Rafael one day saying she had a crippled son that no priest ever allowed to make his First Communion. It would mean very much to her son, who was now 13, if he could go to receive Communion at Mass. They were poor and didn't have a wheel chair. She was a widow but could get someone to carry her son for Mass. I let him make his First Communion. I can still see her tears of joy and his smile. She corresponded with me for a year of two and then we lost contact.

They tell me that the gorgeous beach south of San Rafael, which was totally undeveloped in 1963, now has many fancy hotels. I hope it has improved the lives of the people I knew there.

I spent my two weeks there and discovered something interesting. The sugar companies were the big local employers and were owned by American and British companies. But they paid such low wages to cut sugar cane that the Dominicans who lived there could not afford to work for so little. So the companies imported migrant farm workers (sic!) from the other half of the island, Haitians, who were even poorer and would work for a lower pay! And that, of course, left local Dominicans without work. When will be learn?

I was ashamed of those companies.

But now I found myself also saying Mass and hearing confessions in French (ok – so I struggled!) with the same type of migrant farm workers and migrant housing that I visited so often near Erie and Blissfield, Michigan.

Normally, however our work there was in Spanish. We learned a couple of things: 1) that when the local people were involved, things kept going after we left, like the credit union we started but the people ran. 2) I learned not to bring volunteers along so that the local people had to be involved. When we went to Recife a year later, the word was out that we did not like lay volunteers! Actually I appreciated their help, but it deterred local leadership.

The last person out of there was **Tom Gonzalez**. Tom brought back with him a great young man, **Rafael Jimenez**, a former seminarian there. Rafael stayed in Detroit, married, became a deacon and is very active today in the Church in Southwest Detroit. Tom went to California to help **Cesar Chavez** and is working in that area still today on social justice issues.

I have never returned there. I liked it. I liked the people. I even liked the crowded jitneys that served as buses and taxis, with hens and pigs (they had to ride on the roof) and five people jammed on the front seat. I'll aalways wonder about the folks, the credit union and especially the crippled boy. But life has taken me down other roads.

John Cardinal Dearden

Sending In A Suggestion: South America. Let George Do It. (Have A Drink)

Back in Detroit, when we chatted with other Spanish-speaking priests, it seemed that perhaps our Archdiocese could do <u>something</u> to help out in Latin America. Perhaps the Dominican Republic was not the place. We thought about it.

At that time, our archdiocese had lots of priests. We had one priest for every 7,000 Catholics. South American had one priest for every 70,000 Catholics.

Father John Dewitt took the initiative. I'd like to say I did but he deserves the honor. John, who is now married, has always been an "accomplisher" and was once honored by a national magazine (I think it was *Time*) as one of the most outstanding young clerics in the nation. It was a well worded petition, prepared by John, for all the Spanish-speaking priests of the diocese. We asked **Archbishop Dearden** to assign some priests to work in an archdiocesan mission somewhere in South America. Would he accept? If so, who would he send?

He did. It was me.

I received a call one day in May, 1964 to come in to see the Archbishop. Not knowing the reason, I reviewed mentally all the things I had done wrong, wondering exactly what he knew.

It wasn't that. The Cardinal simply told me that he liked the suggestion and that he thought I would be the best person to open an archdiocesan mission in Latin America. He said it could be anywhere; I could select any diocese in Latin America. I asked if he had any preferences or suggestions. He said he had no preferences. He would suggest, though, three areas. One would be in Panama, near the Chicago mission started by **Fr. Leon Mahon**. A second possibility could be in Caracas, Venezuela; he had already spoken with the auxiliary bishop of Caracas whom he had befriended in Rome at the Vatican Council. The third possibility was in Natal, Brazil, because the Archbishop there was so well known. He told me I could select a companion and travel anywhere to check out possible sites in Latin America.

Well, I was honored to be asked and told him I would accept the assignment. I would get a companion and leave as soon as the school year was out at the seminary (I was still teaching there).

I also left the archbishop's office, and immediately called **Fr. Jim Sheehan** who had an office across the street. I told Jim I needed to talk with him about something important. And, most of all, I needed a drink!

Site Selection With Jim Sheehan

We met in a bar on Michigan Avenue. I had a Manhattan, Jim had a Coca-Cola, and I told him about my meeting with the Archbishop. He agreed to go with me and we actually planned our trip right there. We left the day after classes ended at the seminary.

First stop: Panama City, Panama. We were in luck. We had, as a companion on the plane, **Bishop McGrath**, the bishop of Panama. He was well known and gave us some insights on the political scene there. We left him at the airport and made our way to the parish of St. Miguelito, staffed by three very intelligent and gifted priests. Leo Mahon was the pastor, a priest respected all over for his vision and insights. I knew at once that I didn't want Detroit to be overshadowed by such great minds and successful apostolic work as was found there in San Miguelito. I did decide though, that we had much to learn from Leo and his program.

Leo Mahon gave me several tips: 1) ask for plenty of money annually from Cardinal Dearden. We had to be sure that we had funds to accommodate parish needs, visitors, provide training for the staff and for lay persons, even funds for a vacation away from the hotbed of work; 2) make sure that what we did was a worth-while contribution to the evangelization and missionary efforts in Latin America; 3) always work to attract the men since Latin men were often not involved with the Church. He suggested that I always have beer on hand to serve the men from the parish; 4) he also suggested, that in preparing my report, I give the archbishop three options, two of which should be ridiculous. That way, the cardinal's ego would be taken care of since he would pride himself in selecting the option that made the most sense, which, of course, is what you wanted in the first place.

Leo didn't suggest that I carry gin and tonic for the priests, but I did take note of the good supply he had of both. Limes, too.

Second stop: Caracas, Venezuela. Jim and I had notified **Bishop Henriquez**, the auxiliary bishop, that we were coming, so he was ready for us. He took us for a tour of the city and offered us the choice of two parishes: one was a relatively wealthy, mostly Italian parishioners, the other was a very poor parish with a beautiful church set on the top of a very high hill for all to admire.

The Italian parish was definitely out – I didn't want to work with relatively wealthy Italians – I could do that in Eastpointe, Michigan!

The church on the top of the hill made a great sight but it was sociologically insane to have a church at the top of a mountain, no matter how pretty it looked. People will always come *down* but not always would they be willing (or able in the case of the aged or infirm) to go *up*.

It looked like we had no other alternative in Caracas.

Third Stop: Natal, Brazil: On the way to Natal, the plane stopped at Fortaleza. The airport there is much bigger now. When we landed in 1963, the landing field was not paved, just grass. Men came out and pumped gasoline into our plane using a large hand pump with two men on each side, just like the firemen used to pump water on fires many years ago.

In Natal, the archbishop invited us to stay at their training center about 15 miles out of town but we decided to stay in the heart of the city. We got a hotel room with two beds that only left a foot of space between them and maybe three feet at the bottom. We could hardly walk around.

The archbishop, **Eugênio de Araújo Sales,** (he later was promoted to Rio de Janeiro and made a cardinal), was friendly but quite "stiff". His car was driven by a driver and the archbishop sat alone in the back seat wearing the wide brimmed Roman style cleric hat. He looked aloof. His diocese was highly organized and efficient. They had a wonderful education system by radio which was set up following **Paulo Freire's** system of "conscientization".

(They used the teaching of literacy to expose the adult students to their human rights, thus they "conscientized" the people – the new military government soon shut that down and exiled Paulo Freire.)

The Vatican Council documents allowed bishops to set up "experimental" parishes that could adapt the liturgical and catechetical approaches to the needs and culture of the people. One of our goals was to be as innovative a parish as allowed. However, when I spoke to the director of the radio education system, which was a very large program, he told Jim and me how the archbishop controlled every little item in the diocese – saying, "I can't order a waste paper basket without written approval from the archbishop!"

That was enough. I surely did not want to work under such a leader.

Fourth stop: Recife, Brazil: To stop in Recife was our own idea, and we had told Cardinal Dearden of this before we left. **Dom Helder Camara** was the Archbishop of Recife, a shipping seaport of over a million and a half inhabitants. He was a short man with a slight build but he was an extremely vocal advocate of justice for the poor. From the moment I met him, I liked him and often compared him to Father Clement Kern.

I have to tell you two things about our arrival in Recife. Jim Sheehan had always been a man with a large bone structure, and spent many years gaining weight and losing weight, only to gain again. This summer he was his healthiest heftiness. We hailed a taxi with our luggage. The next cab in line was a tiny Volkswagen "bug", with the passenger seat removed from the front and thus only room for two people in the back seat. Jim stuck his leg in and tried to double over to get into the back seat. With his size, it didn't work at first. He tried from different angles. Meanwhile the taxi driver is laughing out loud. With a couple of unpriestly exclamations, Jim slid headfirst into the car. We all laughed. (Jim, who is one of my best friends, has considerably slimmed down today to a mere shadow of his former self.)

The second humorous thing was our hotel room. After the 8' by 8' room in Natal, we decided that might be the size of all Brazilian hotel rooms. As we checked into our Recife Hotel, we cleverly asked for a "large suite". (We did realize that the archdiocese was paying.) We must have gotten the Presidential Suite or its equivalent. Jim had a bedroom and bath on the east end; I had the same on the west side. In the middle was a parlor fit to have a large party! We felt like we were two farm boys arriving in New York City!

(Not that I have anything against farm boys, you understand...)

Dom Helder had inherited the "Archbishop's Palace", a large, old, not well maintained building on, perhaps, an area of three or four acres. It was two stories, with his living quarters upstairs and on the first floor were all the offices for the archdiocese and its programs. The hallway on the first floor was filled with people either waiting to see Dom Helder (they would be brought upstairs for that) or to see someone in one of the other offices. It reminded me of the crowded hall of Most Holy Trinity Parish in Detroit, especially on Thursday night.

It was such an honor to sit and chat with **Dom Helder**. It felt like I was talking with **Dorothy Day** or **Mother Teresa** or **Father Kern**. (All of the same saintly mold of dedication to the poor and to justice!)

Dom Helder Camara
Archbishop of Recife

With a twinkle in his eye and with the impetuosity of an urgent man, Dom Helder delighted us by telling us two things. First, he immediately assured us that we could do any experimentation we needed to do in the parish, saying, "As long as you are helping our people, feel free to do whatever you think will help!" Secondly, he simply said, let's get in my car and I will show you the parishes I have in mind for you.

Dom Helder took us to visit two parishes. The first parish was in a lower middle class area near the University of Pernambuco. (Pernambuco was the name of the state.)The second one, on the western side of town, in the sector called "*Casa Amarela*" ("Yellow house'), was in a very poor area called "*Nova Descoberta*" ("the new discovery").

Nova Descoberta was perfect. It had one main street running between seven high hills (called "morros") with somewhere between 40,000 and 50,000 inhabitants. (They say there are 70,000 today.) It had one entrance to the whole area from town and was crawling with people filling the streets. Sociologically, and from an organizer's point of view, it was ideal.

Jim Sheehan and I were convinced that we had found the right place and the right archbishop.

We left Recife and headed for Rio de Janeiro from where we would travel to Petropolis, once the capitol of the Portugese Empire. This was in 1815, when the Emperor Prince John, had fled to Brazil out of fear of Napoleon whose troops had entered Portugal. It was here that there was a language school that prepared missionaries to work in Brazil, teaching them Portugese, Brazilian history and Latin American sociology. Freire Joao, the director, said the classes started in two weeks on the first of July, but they were completely filled. He said I could apply for the classes that would begin in seven months (the following January).

Sure. Like I didn't know politics. Two weeks later, I was there as a student.

Presentation to Archbishop Dearden

Jim Sheehan and I returned to Detroit and wrote our report. We discretely presented the findings of our trip in our report and observed that there were several options that could be chosen. Now that I look back, two of the options look slightly inane. The third was to opt for establishing our archdiocesan mission in the parish of Our Lady of Lourdes in Nova Descoberta in Recife and to send me immediately to the language school in Petropolis, to support us with at least $25,000 a year (according to the attached budget) and to allow three priests to be assigned there, the other two to be selected by me.

The Cardinal, in his wisdom, selected the third option. He said that he would start off with only two priests. He asked me if I had anyone in mind. I told him I wanted Father Mike Jorissen, a young priest whose work with the migrant farm workers showed tremendous insight, zeal and dedication.

At first the cardinal resisted sending a priest that "new", but when I mentioned that I might reconsider my willingness to head the mission if he was going to assign "second class" priests, he immediately agreed with my suggested choice. I didn't mean to be arrogant, but at that time, my mind was really set on Mike Jorissen.

Leaving: Classmate Party

That meant that I really had two weeks to pack up, get inoculated, get a "Permanent Resident Visa" from the Brazilian Consulate in Chicago and get down to Petropolis in Brazil.

I wanted to say goodbye to my priest friends and classmates, but time was too short and no one who heard about it thought of giving me a going-away party (very few people did hear).

I asked a Trinity parishioner to call all of my classmates and tell them there was a "Farewell" luncheon for me at Stouffer's Restaurant in the Eastland mall next Thursday. (I had never before planned a party for myself, but I did want to see them before I left.)

Next I met with Father Mike Jorissen and we started to develop our "Plan".

Downtown Recife, Pernambuco, Brazil

Recife: The Big Plan

Recife was a large city with many problems. It was a hotbed for communist activity. A modern city, it still had the majority of the population living in poverty. The Church was trying to help the people with limited resources.

We wanted a different approach in our missionary endeavors in Brazil. If we did the same as everyone else had been doing for years, the two of us would not help the situation in Latin America one bit. A drop in the bucket. Things would go on the same way. Our approach <u>had</u> to be different.

Here is what we came up with:
> Our effort had to contribute by way of <u>a new approach</u> – not repeating or imitating what is done in the United States with emphasis on school and children, but should aim at *empowering adults*, especially married couples.

> We wanted our work to be <u>in a large, urban area</u> where the decisions towards change would be made, for or against communism, revolt, etc.

> We would <u>use a team approach</u> where the opinions of all would be respected and considered and *decisions made by consensus*, not by majority vote.

> We would use <u>experimental teaching techniques</u> which had proven effective with people whose intelligence we respected but who lacked sufficient education to be considered literate.

> We would <u>not use lay volunteers</u> from the United States since our goal was to *develop local parish leadership*.

> We would start <u>our own version of the Cursillo</u> (we called it "Fermento", which in English means "yeast" in which we would add a social action and social consciousness dimension. Our "Cursillo", unlike those in other Latin American nations, would be controlled by poor persons, not the wealthy! We would <u>live poorly</u> to identify with the people we served.

> We would <u>not take part in revolutionary activities</u> since we were guests in that country, but would encourage people to *speak out against injustices*.

> We would <u>not "go native"</u> since everyone knew we were Americans; we would simply recognize the fact that we were adding on to our life experiences and knowledge as we acculturated to the Brazilian "ambience".

> We would be part of the local archdiocesan scene and <u>collaborate with our fellow Brazilian priests and nuns</u> and participate in Catholic Action, retreats and the local Pastoral Plan. (Every parish had a pastoral plan, usually painted on the wall!)

> We would <u>adapt the liturgy</u> to meet the needs of the people.

Some clippings from <u>The Michigan Catholic</u> and
<u>The Detroit Free Press</u> when we left for Recife

The Start-Up Schedule

I was able to attend CENFI for my language and cultural training. CENFI is short for *"Centro de Formacao Intercultural"*, Portuguese for the *"Center of Intercultural Formation"*. I loved it. Like a paid tropical vacation with fifty dedicated people, lay persons, nuns, religious brothers, and priests, from United States, Canada, Italy, France, Holland and Germany.

I formed really close friendships with the team of priests and lay people from the diocese of Saskatoon,

Saskatchewan, Canada. **Fr. Bernard I. Dunn** is back in Canada and remains in touch with me today; **Fr. Bob "Tex" Ogle** returned, became an outstanding Member of Parliament in Ottawa and died a few years ago of cancer. They took over a parish in the interior of the state of Alagoas, southwest of Recife some 150 miles. I was very touched one day when he called from Ottawa saying he had a terminal illness and wanted to visit me and each of his friends before he died. When Tex came, he told me he thought his life was extended for a few years simply from the inspiration he got from reading a paperback book entitled, "*Getting Well Again*". (As a result, I started buying copies of that book to give to anyone I knew who might have a terminal illness. I have probably given out forty of those books.)

My companion, **Fr. Mike Jorissen**, had to finish the summer serving migrant farm workers in the area around Imlay City, Michigan. We decided since he couldn't enter CENFI until January, that he could tour South America visiting outstanding parishes just to get contacts and ideas that would help us in our work. He did more than that; he spent some time with some very outstanding theologians in Columbia, Peru and Chile, forming friendships that continued to bring ideas to our parish.

Mike joined me at the parish in Recife in mid-December. We celebrated our first Christmas with the people. I still remember it. We had midnight Mass on top of a hill so more people could attend. After Mass, until the wee hours, families went from house to house paying social visits. Not too much liquor, just Kool-Aid and cookies and genuine friendship. Life is so real with poor people and has a charm all its own.

After Christmas, we returned to Detroit for six days to have a grand send off and "commissioning" at the Blessed Sacrament Cathedral on Woodward Avenue in Detroit.

When we left Detroit, I went alone to work in our parish and Mike went to CENFI for four, almost five months of training.

Recife: Where is God? Why Am I Here? Alone!

It was during that period of time that I went though a real traumatic few weeks. Perhaps the "lowest" point in my life.

I could speak Portuguese, sure, but not like a native. And I certainly didn't grasp everything said at meetings, when several spoke rapidly at once. With hardly ever speaking English, my brain just tired every single day, as I struggled to speak and understand what was initially very foreign. I think I can do better today, almost forty years later!

Depression began to set in. Then questions. How did I ever end up here? What am I supposed to be doing here?

I even started to question my religion. Or any religion for that matter. God? Christ? The Mass? The Catholic Church? I questioned them all. Sometimes I was awake most of the night.

Slowly, bit by bit I started to piece everything together. It wasn't easy, though, because through all this I was smiling and saying Mass and preaching.

I figured, just as I had learned, that the world is so infinitely well planned, from the tiniest atom to the grandiosity of many galaxies and universes that only a Superior Being could think it up. No human brain could plan this world. There had to be a God. Surely, in all of history, with every tribe and nation, 99% of the world has always believed in a Superior Being.

Okay, there had to be a God.

What about Christ? I slowly figured that out, too. We humans are sinful at times, and we have thereby offended our God who calls us to holiness. No person could never atone for all the sins of our fellow human beings. That was it: God sent His Son to redeem us. It had to be!

Once I came back to Christ, I traced the Catholic Church from Peter to the present. With all its faults, it has endured through emperors and dictators, czars and presidents. You have to love it!

So after a couple of agonizing weeks, all alone in the midst of 40,000 people hustling around me, I found peace within myself and joy in why I was there.

I had finished many years of seminary training. That, together with my family support, gave me a solid footing in my Faith. This short period of questioning turned out to be healthy for me. I have never doubted since, which has been a real blessing. He even did more. God seemed to send me, at the end of this "trial", a special man, "**Joao Noventa**".

Joao Noventa Was Going To Kill Me

I was new. I also was predisposed to like alcoholics, from my work on Skid Row. Alcoholics, for the most part, are nice, sentimentalists to a fault, and usually harmless. Besides, I discovered, they liked to be kidded. Perhaps life has been otherwise too solemn and sad for them so a smile goes a long way.

With that in mind, you would easily understand that I had befriended the local alcoholic who actively meandered around, in a happy, care-free way each evening in front of our church. Some might say he was drunk. Anyway, I grew to like him and often chatted with him.

Then, someone told me my new alcoholic friend was in jail for just a minor thing.

I decided to go visit him in jail, which I always did in my other parishes. This was Brazil, however, and it was different. The custom was that the police would immediately release anyone who was visited by the priest!

Like I say, I was new.

Now it so happened that the person who had him put in jail was a man by the name of **Joao Noventa**. Joao liked to think he was tough (you, I'm sure know the type). He never had anything to do with religion. He ran several houses of prostitution (small time, poverty style). He was macho in ways I don't want to mention here.

And Joao was angry. At me!! I let that no good get out of jail right after Joao had him put there. Joao announced to one and all that he <u>would kill the new priest</u>.

To say the least, I was a little unsettled when I heard this news. Forget about depression. Now my energy was "revved" up, although I wasn't sure for what. But I carried on, slightly more watchful as I climbed the hills.

I was returning from downtown Recife and just entering our main (and only) street. It was at least 110 degrees of heat in the sun. The street was, as usual, crowded with pedestrians but I immediately managed to spot one person in particular – Joao Noventa.

Should I offer him a ride? It was about a mile yet to go – he lived up the hill behind my house, I had found out.

Then, I thought, if I snub him and drive by in our Jeep, will he hate me even more?

I stopped and offered Joao a ride. He refused. I offered again. He refused. When I offered the third time he jumped in, never nodding or saying one word. I think he felt ashamed to be seen chatting with this "*%#*" priest. I tried to act friendly and pass the time. He bolted out when we reached the church, never speaking. I had no idea what was going through his mind or whether he was racing up the hill to get a gun from his house.

Following **Fr. Leon Mahon's** advice (he was the Chicago priest working in Panama), I had stocked up with three cases of beer in my house. That was so that I could offer the men a drink when they came around. (I have never been much of a beer drinker, myself, preferring a "Club Manhattan" for real celebrations.)

Sometime after 11 p.m. that evening, there was a clap outside my front door. (Brazilians clap their hands instead of ringing doorbells.) When I peeked out and saw it was Joao I didn't know what to expect. Joao had come to apologize! He said he was sorry. He would never kill me. We became friends that night over a couple of beers.

From that day forward, for the next two years, Joao was my best advocate and protector. If he heard someone waking me for a sick call at 2 a.m., he would grab his flashlight and dress, come down the hill and insist and going with me to make sure nothing would happen to me.

Joao brought me out of any depression from that day forward. I knew we would succeed. I still miss him.

Joao has given up his houses of prostitution and some other shady things he had going. I was proud of him. However, **Father Bob Singelyn,** who is pastor there now tells me he never sees Joao around the church these days.

The Faces Are Still There But Not The Names

I can still picture so many of the people in the parish, but I have trouble remembering their names! **Dom Julio** was an elderly man who served as president of our parish conference of St. Vincent de Paul. His group ran classes for women in sewing, distributed large amounts of free food and clothing (which we received free from the *Catholic Relief Services* in the United States) and astonishingly, built a simple adobe home, from scratch every Sunday for one of the many widows. (Widows in Brazil usually were desperately poor, since they had no pensions or Social Security to assist them,)

I was very impressed by one elderly man who took the Gospel serious when he heard about "not approaching the altar until you have reconciled with your brother". He took a long trip on one of the old buses into the interior to make up with his own brother and then returned to Recife to go to confession and receive Holy Communion at Mass in our parish. **Luis and Jenni** lived just the other side of the parish church (near the ladies I later discovered were prostitutes). They were a delightful young couple that helped quite a bit in the parish. Our sacristan was a very thin widow by the name of **Dona Maria**. The brother of Carminha, who headed our catechetical program was **Antonio.** Antonio had "muscles" and was responsible for bending and shaping the iron rods which were used to reinforce the cement when we built the convent. **Oscar Gomes da Silva** and **Severino (Bio) da Silva** were great aids in the parish.

We had a great doctor and a good dentist. The parishioners were so poor they seldom saw a real doctor or a real dentist. There were all kinds of amateurs working for a low cost. Amateur "dentists" advertised that they would pull all your teeth for free if you purchased your false teeth from them. One young girl in the parish, who had a beautiful smile with solid teeth, appeared one day with a terrible-looking set of false teeth. She had had a cavity which abscessed, so she went to one of these amateurs and had all her teeth pulled!

We had many seminarians stay in the parish as part of their training at the grass roots level. It meant a lot to the people and I am certain was valuable training for the seminarians.

Agreement Between The Two Archdioceses

Cardinal Dearden had given me a couple dozen sheets of his personal embossed stationery and told me to write up some sort of agreement between the two archdioceses. He thought there should be something in writing that we would agree to staff the parish with at least two priests. I asked the Cardinal how many years should the agreement cover. He said, "Oh, make it for one hundred years. We'll both be dead and no one will even know about it by that time!" So I wrote the agreement and had both men sign it. (It also left me some good stationery to have fun with later!)

Recife: Getting Nuns – Selecting, Convent, Water

We wanted to have some nuns down there working with us. Because I had several relatives in the Monroe, Michigan, religious order called the *Sisters, Servants of the Immaculate Heart of Mary*, or "IHM" sisters, I approached them first. I had that order teach me in grade school at Gesu School in Detroit and had worked with them at Most Holy Trinity Parish.

It took nerve but I went to see **Mother Anna Marie Grix, IHM**, the Mother General, who was the head of the congregation of approximately 1,800 women at that time.

I asked her if she would appoint four or five nuns to work with us in that special parish apostolate. If possible, I said, select your *best superior*, your *holiest nun*, your *most creative* nun, your smartest, *most intellectual nun*, and finally, a *nun who could do anything*, from mechanics to carpentry. She laughed. I don't know how the four were selected. I do know that the four women who joined us there were extremely capable. I am convinced to this day that they could run General Motors!

She, however, had some stipulations. I had to build them a decent convent and the convent had to have running water for showers and toilets. She would not let me know her final decision, however, until after she made a personal visit. She didn't want to say she'd send some women without feeling comfortable with the setting

The construction of the convent was another interesting story. I designed it originally and needed the signature of a registered architect. I took the design to an American company working in Brazil and they said they would ask one of their architects to "improve" my drawings before he would sign off. A week later I had a whole set of professional drawings, for free, along with the comment that said, "If the builders had followed your design, this convent would have been only eleven inches long!"

Dr. Roberto, who owned all the property in Nova Descoberta, said he would let us use a section of land beside and to the rear of the church. (Many old wealthy families in Latin America were reluctant to give up land, so they simply collected rent from everyone who lived on their land. Dr. Roberto boasted that he owned one-seventh of Recife.) There was a 3-family dwelling on the property at that time which needed to be torn down, but only after we paid the three families to move. Usually, you would pay them the equivalent of three months rent.

Once I was assured that the nuns would come, I spoke to the head of the Recife Water Department to ask for a special water line to be run down to the convent, just for the nuns. I had a note from Dom Helder, the archbishop, to intercede for this cause. That, together with the fact the water department director had been trained by the Detroit Water Department while my Dad was mayor, were determining facts in getting water for the convent.

Next, I assembled a construction crew made up of parishioners. I had asked to meet some of them and found a man, a "dynamo", who pled with me to make him the construction superintendent. He said he knew who the good workers were and who weren't so good. He would select and do an excellent job. If he succeeded, he said, he could rise in the trade and be a construction superintendent anywhere. I chose him and did not regret it. That convent is so well built it would probably withstand a nuclear bomb! (I might be exaggerating, not lying…)

By the time Mother Anna Marie gave me her decision, it was April. Getting the plans approved and water assured took almost two months. The nuns were on their way to CENFI starting in July and would arrive in the parish in early December. It took almost two months to get the families out and to tear down the existing building. That left about 13 weeks to start and finish the construction. I asked the local union to give me a list of their "going rates" for each category of construction workers and told my "superintendent" to pay our crew 15% higher than union wages. I also told them they would be paid for 15 weeks guaranteed so if they finished the building ahead, they could look for other work and have extra money in their pockets. They finished in ten weeks.

The Mother General; Shots Ring Out, Urination

As I said, **Mother Anna Marie** had to see the place first. She arrived with her companion, **Sr. Thomas Acquinas Wellesley**, in February, 1965 for a visit. For some reason I was nervous. She accompanied me as we walked around the parish. She had on the "old" style habit, which was lovely but also very warm in that heat. (That is probably why she readily approved an adaptation in the habit they wore before the sisters left Monroe, along with the fact that she had made a Cursillo and was now enthusiastic about a mission to Latin America.)

Everything went well until after she finished lunch with me and some "leading" parishioners, including Joao Noventa. at our house near the church. We were going to get in our Jeep and visit the archbishop. As we stepped out the front door, a young man, probably twelve years old, was urinating into the ditch some twelve feet in front of us. I hesitated and chatted to distract the nuns. All of a sudden I heard two loud gunshots and at the same time two bullets hit the front wall of my house, not five feet from the nuns. I ushered everyone back into the house. Joao Noventa, however, ran across the street to the spot where an inebriated man was waving a revolver. Joao wrestled the gun away from him, bawled the man out and yelled to me that it was okay to come out.

God is good. All this seemingly had no effect on the decision of Mother Anna Marie to send the nuns. In March, she explained the project to all of the members of the community asking for volunteers. I don't know how many volunteered but she did name four wonderfully qualified sisters. They were:

> **Mary Louise (Vincent Mary) DeBaldo, Superior**
> **Dorothy (Mary Seton) Diederichs**
> **Gertrude (Marie Bosco) O'Leary**
> **Judy (Helena) Woods**

Recife: Dom Helder Camara

I loved Dom Helder, our archbishop. Like Father Kern in so many ways, he was a saint of the poor and defender of the cause of justice. I was thrilled several times to help him prepare the English translation of speeches that he was asked to give in the United States.

But I have to tell you a story that showed what kind of a man he was. He shunned the external signs of his membership in the hierarchy of the Catholic Church. I never saw any purple; he wore a simple black or a white cassock with a wooden, not gold or bejeweled, cross. He lived a very simple life style. He was more open than any bishop I ever met, exemplified by his confiding in all his diocesan and order priests at a large meeting about his being investigated three times by Curia members from the Vatican!

Here is the story I love: Our area, Nova Descoberta, had very few homes that had running water among the approximately 40,000 people. We only had a few homes with the equivalent of "outhouses". As a result, the crowded hillsides, especially in the heat of day, often carried odors that many "cultured" people would shy away from! A heavy rain often resolved that problem. It was like the whole area took a refreshing bath.

Except for the large open gutter that runs along the street where everything unwanted, good and bad, seemed to end up as it headed for one of the rivers.

The problem came when the ditch became damned up because of so much debris at the entrance to our area. Father Mike Jorissen suggested that we recruit our men to clear the way. We used our influence to get 100 shovels from the city and we hired a couple of trucks that would carry away these stinking loads to a dump.

What a great idea! Of course, as a holy priest, I assumed that I would supervise and oversee this operation, watching carefully to see that it was well done. Sure…

Before we even started, the archbishop, **Dom Helder Camara**, who had heard about this project, showed up. He grabbed a shovel and led the men as they started digging this (ugh!!) smelly stuff and tossing it into trucks. Mike Jorissen was already there. Obviously, I was soon in there and we all worked until the ditch was clear enough for the water to flow once again.

All this time, I kept wondering how many archbishops around the world would have gotten into that ditch. Or how long they would have stayed. Or how many of my priest friends would have joined in the shoveling.

Dom Helder was at ease with himself as a fellow human being. No pretense. Seven years later, when I was married and had small children, I went to hear him talk when he was in Detroit. He saw me get out of my car from a half block away and actually ran all the way to give me one of his famous hugs (called "abrazo"). Again, I wondered how many archbishops would shed "dignity" to run and greet a friend.

Not that all priests and archbishops aren't saints, you understand. It's just that there are very few like Dom Helder Camara!

Investigations By Rome

Dom Helder told all his priests that the conservative military government in Brazil (they had revolted and taken over the year I arrived in 1964) was making accusations against him, from time to time, to the Vatican authorities in Rome. There were three current accusations: 1) he was heretical, preaching in Protestant churches; 2) he had sponsored an immoral, wild event on the sacred grounds of the archbishop's palace; 3) he was encouraging subversives.

Dom Helder explained that 1) since he felt the Church was losing the youth, he would sponsor a free dance with the best local band on the never used back yard of the "palace". Over a thousand young people attended and he had a chance to talk with them and motivate them. It was not a wild party, he told us. 2) He did speak in more than one Protestant church, he said, in the spirit of ecumenism and not as a heretic. 3) He did say that he would always talk about justice and point out injustices. Some, more conservative members of the military might think of this as subversive.

As a result of the accusations, the Vatican (for the third time) was sending the Assistant to Cardinal Octavianni to investigate these charges. This investigator would arrive on a Thursday evening. Dom Helder asked that we all return that Thursday evening when he would host a reception. At that time we could show our support for Dom Helder, publicly and privately. It would be held in a nearby parish hall. He also encouraged us to "please wear your cassocks!" since many of us had abandoned the habit of wearing the heavy cassocks in that heat.

That Thursday night, Mike Jorissen was out of town with the Jeep, so I donned my cassock and rode on the back of **Father Adriano's** Honda motor scooter to the hall. It was dark with no sign of life. We turned around and headed for the archbishop's palace. It was dark, but there were a couple of lights on upstairs in Dom Helder's quarters. We clapped and I shouted "Dom Helder!!"

Dom Helder appeared on the balcony and I shouted to him, "It's George and Adriano. We're here. What happened to the reception? We even have our cassocks on!"

Oops. It was then that I noticed that the "investigator" was standing next to him. Me and my big mouth!

The next day, a messenger arrived from Dom Helder inviting me to join him and the investigator for lunch in a downtown restaurant. It seems the chancery had called all the parishes that had telephones, but Adriano's parish and ours had no phone. The big reception had to be cancelled. The investigator turned out to be a very open monsignor, originally from the Netherlands, and the charges against Dom Helder were dropped.

Aside: The Powerful Mystique Of Faith

Dom Helder did give me a small insight that I want to pass on to you. He told me that I should never forget the power of the certain "mystique" that religion gives to humans. "Be a good citizen" and other platitudes will never move people to heroic acts. Only religion and faith will do that.

Look at the saints. I was always impressed at what St. Ignatius of Loyola reportedly said to the rich and worldly student in Paris, Francis Xavier, "What does it profit a man to gain the whole world and suffer the loss of his soul?" After that, Francis changed his life and became a saint and one of the most successful missionaries for Christ in the history of the Church.

It is difficult to define "mystique" – it is a spiritual motivating force that brings humans to act, often heroically, for their God and their religion.

Look at people like **Gandhi, Mother Teresa, Dorothy Day, Martin Luther King Jr.** – they were tremendously moved by their beliefs and they knew how to use the mystique of religion to motive and inspire others.

I often wonder if our Church leaders today fully understand the power they have by using our Faith to motivate people to great holiness, to bring about peace and justice in our world.

The Work

We tried to follow the "Plan". We tried. That living poorly idea was good except for carrying our own water every day for the first year. That's when I realized how much water we use every day and how heavy water is when it is you that is carrying it.

From then on, when I saw people carrying water in the parish, I really felt for them!

The first Sunday that I was there, we had over 300 youngsters make their First Communion. Most of them I never saw in church again. I resolved to check on the system of preparing children for the sacraments and discovered it was done in the public schools by teachers who were more into "voodoo" than into the Catholic religion. I was shocked that they were preparing children in the Catholic religion speaking out of the abysmal depths of their own ignorance. I met with them and changed that real soon, appointing practicing and knowledgeable parishioners to teach the Faith in our own catechism classes.

I noticed that we hardly had any men between the age of 14 and 60 attending Mass on Sunday. We celebrated Mass in four locations in the parish. So I had everyone at Mass one Sunday just write on a piece of paper their name, age and what hill they lived on.

I could tell from their name what sex they were since boys' names ended usually with the letter "o" and girls' names normally with the letter "a". By graphing the hills and putting an "x" for each person from that hill, I could easily see what areas of the parish we were affecting and which needed some work. At that time, I could see that almost no one went to Mass from a large populated area known as the "Correigo de Areia" ("the corridor of sand"). We soon did a lot of home visiting and *Family of God* evening meetings in that area.

But the shocking revelation of the lack of adult men was worse that I had anticipated. Absolutely not one adult male between 14 and 65 came to Mass! A lot of little boys came. Many old men, probably "cramming for the finals", came to church. Mike and I, along with the nuns had a lot to do.

Dom Helder, our archbishop, was pleased when I laid out our "Plan" before him, explaining how we intended to form conscientious leaders through our own system of experientially-based catechism, followed by the Cursillo type retreat. Dom Helder wisely cautioned me that, while we zeroed in on the development of individuals, we cannot lose the masses. We must include in our plan, exactly how we intended to reach the masses of people in our area. He did it by radio.

We decided to plan an approach to the masses of people in Nova Descoberta on the big feasts – Christmas, Easter, Palm Sunday, etc. Instead of holding Mass inside the church on these days, we would have processions and have Mass in the middle of a big field in the Correigo de Areia atop the bed of a truck with loudspeakers all over, or have Midnight Mass on Christmas on top of the highest hill, sometimes in conjunction with an adjoining parish.

On two Palm Sundays, I rode a dirty burro from one end of the street through the parish while Mike rode a burro from the other end. That was very impressive. Except for one thing. The first year that we had Palm Sunday Mass in the church, I had told the people how the crowd had followed Jesus that first Palm Sunday. However, the crowd was smart. They knew there had to be over a thousand people and that the church would only hold 250. About five hundred feet from the church there was a mad rush towards the front doors, leaving one stunned priest alone on a slowly moving, slightly frightened, dirty donkey.

The next year, we had the Mass in an open area in Correigo de Areia.

And I had someone bathe the donkeys.

On Buying Milk

When we were first in Recife, the couple that helped us the most were **Luis and Carminha**. Luis was hired to help in the construction of the convent. I remember how he always wore the same shirt to work, careful hung it on a nail while he worked bareback in the heat. He wore the same shirt to church on Sunday (it had red, white and blue stripes, if you must know). I kidded him about it. Then, one day, he said to me, "Father, I only own one shirt!"

Geez. I never knew a man that only owned one shirt. How many men do you know like that?

We were having meetings of "married couples" (this was part of our plan). I noticed that one week Luis would come without Carminha. The next week Carminha would come without Luis. I finally asked them why. Carminha explained, "Father, we only own one pair of thong sandals! We would be embarrassed to come barefooted to a parish meeting."

I had so much to learn.

Carminha gave birth to a new baby. They could not afford to buy milk. Many Brazilian mothers bought boxes of powdered milk to give their children, but because of their poverty, would water it down too much and their babies did not get all the vitamins they needed.

So Mike and I decided to buy milk for Luis and Carminha's baby. They lived in a house on the hill right behind our house. There was a man who walked his cow down our street every day and who would sell the cow's milk "on tap", as it were. You had to provide a container, a bottle or can of any sort. We would buy a bottle each day, take a little for our cereal and send the rest up to Carminha. The problem was that, when no one was watching, the "milkman" would add water to the cow's milk, just to stretch it a bit. Every so often he would add too much water and the milk and water would separate in the bottle. I took such a bottle back to him on the street. He just laughed and said, "Well, you caught me this time!" He gave me my money back for that bottle.

When I look back, I remember that the water there was not healthy water. You had to boil it and then filter it to know you could drink it safely. I shutter to think of the people who might have gotten ill drinking that watered down milk.

A photo of the original team in January, 1966 shortly after the arrival of the nuns, when Bishop Joe Schoenherr and Father Bill Carolin visited us. The veils were the first to go as the nuns adapted their garb. Left to right, they are Bishop Schoenherr, Sr. Gertrude (Marie Bosco) O'Leary, Fr. Carolin, Sr. Mary Louise (Vincent Mary) DeBaldo, Superior, Sr. Judy (Helena) Woods, Fr. Mike Jorissen, Sr. Dorothy (Mary Seton) Diederichs, and Fr. George Van Antwerp.

Side Note On Quaintness Before Knowing People

I remember noting when I first arrived how rugged people were as they carried water up the hills, usually on their head. I noted especially a very elderly woman who carried water up different hills almost all day, as long as the public spigots were open. It looked so quaint.

How "ugly American" that judgment was.

I got to know that elderly woman. I knew her by name. I knew that she was a penniless widow, and that she suffered from rheumatism and arthritis. That it was extremely painful for her to carry those heavy loads and to climb those dirt "steps" up the hills. (People carved out steps, but they were often washed away and, when it rained, were very slippery and dangerous.) But this elderly woman earned the equivalent of one American penny for every five gallon can of water she carried up the hill, serving someone who was also poor. It was those pennies that permitted this woman to buy food to eat.

I had gotten to know many men on Skid Row as individual human beings. Similarly, every day as I came know more and more of the people in Nova Descoberta, I appreciated them and admired them more. Sometimes, I still feel like crying when I picture those I was honored to know. Such good and talented people, so much intelligence wasted for lack of education, so much preventable illness and premature deaths, all kinds of injustices – it makes me wonder how you and I can get involved to make this world a little bit better.

Mike Jorissen: Great Ideas; Probing Preacher

You should get to know Mike Jorissen, my priestly co-worker in Brazil. He is now married to a wonderful women (Gerry Verdun) and selling real estate in Texas.

Mike is a thinker. Very Intelligent. Most of the good ideas we had in our "Plan" came from Mike. He always had great ideas.

But his sermons were the very best. When he preached, he never said anything unless he was convinced that it was worth saying. His style was based on the fact that he believed that the audience in church was intelligent. So he spoke in such a way that they could reason things out and come to conclusions on their own. I would sit on the side when Mike preached and just be entranced by what he said and how he said it. Few preachers that I have ever heard had such an involving manner of speaking, and I have heard many sermons!

Mike was always honest and forthright in dealing with people. When the people would come to us to ask us to intercede for them with the government, Mike would ask, "Why do you come to us?" People would respond, "Because the officials will listen to the priest and not to us". Mike told them so many times, "If the priest keeps interceding for you, the government will never listen to you!" "You have to keep going there, pestering them, until they finally listen to you."

It's hard to believe but Mike, mostly using that leadership, with the added enthusiasm the people received from the Cursillo (that we called "Fermento"), inspired the people to go down themselves in groups. The next thing we knew the city was paving steps up each hill. Then, the city started putting street light up the hills. I was amazed! Mike had empowered people to demand services for the area. It was a good feeling.

Voice From The Casket or How To Receive A Nun's Final Vows

The youngest nun, Judy Woods, had not made her "final vows" which normally are made before the superior of the religious order, in this case **Mother Anna Marie Grix, IHM**, in Monroe, Michigan. This would mean a trip back to the States. Judy wanted to take her vows here in front of the people she was working with. I told her I could get permission to "receive" her final vows from the superior and from the archbishop in Detroit.

(I didn't need the archbishop's permission, but I did have his personal stationery and had a plan in mind. So I secretly typed up a letter addressed to me from the archbishop giving me permission to receive her vows and instructing me on how the ceremony should be conducted. I waited for the opportune time, a day when I would receive in the mail a letter from the archdiocese so

I could use the envelope with a recent Detroit posting date.)

The perfect opportunity came. All of us were going out to a restaurant to celebrate a birthday when we stopped at the main Recife Post Office, where we had a post office box. I had them wait in the Jeep – the four nuns and Mike – while I went in for our mail. Sure enough, there was a letter from the Archdiocese of Detroit. I carefully opened it, removed its content and substituted my fake letter, resealing the envelope.

When I got to the car, I handed the mail to the nuns in the back seat and told them to look through it while I headed for the restaurant, "*Copo do Leite*" ("Cup of Milk").

"Here's a letter from the archbishop!"

"Read it", I said.

The first page I made sound very reasonable and harmless although I did say the "candidate" should be dressed in white as appropriate for "the bride of Christ", using a phrase that I knew Judy disliked!

But on the second page I gave wild ideas. She should lower herself into a wooden casket, symbolizing death to self. The congregation would shout "Rise up! Rise up! Rise up!" three times. At this point she would rise out of the casket. Trumpets would sound. This would symbolize she has risen with the Lord.

There was more, but I guess I have forgotten the rest. I didn't mean to be blasphemous, and once, the nuns saw it all, we had a good laugh.

Judy did make her final vows and the archbishop of Recife was with us for the occasion.

Can Never Forget Irma Magna

"Irma" is the Portugese equivalent for "sister" and is used as the title for women religious.

Irma Magna was the name of an outstanding woman religious who operated a program near the far end of the parish. Irma Magna was starting to get old; she definitely was past "middle age". She had wonderful programs there for women and for children in a very nice, substantial building erected by her order. All by herself, she operated that program for many years. In my mind, she deserved a lot of respect for the work she did. We celebrated Mass in her center once a week. I cannot write about our parish there without paying a small tribute to that outstanding religious, whose presence in this world might otherwise be forgotten.

Other priests: the OMIs, Msgr. Osvaldo, the Dutch priests (Adriano)

We really liked the other priests in the area.

I won't give his name, since he was later killed by the secret police when they tried to annoy Dom Helder. He was a Brazilian priest who became a good friend of mine. We traveled together to attend the ordination of a new priest in Maceio, Alagoas (120 miles south of Recife). The newly ordained priest had been a seminarian who spent several months helping in Nova Descoberta.

Father Adriano was a happy-go-lucky Dutch missionary who was stationed in the parish just west of us, on the other side of the hill. Their church was owned by the nearby cotton mill factory. It was clean, had velvet covered padding on the kneelers and was so nice it could fit into any well-to-do American suburb! Two priests were stationed there and lived across a plaza from the church in a home that originally belonged to the factory owner.

There were dozens of factory-owned housing units nearby for workers to rent. Because the church was so nice and the priests lived in such a fancy home, their weekly collections were very low, averaging about the equivalent of nine American dollars a week. That is all the priests had to eat on. (We tried to live poorly and told the people they should be supporting us. When I left there two years later, our weekly collections were up to an amount equal to nineteen American dollars. I felt good about that.)

The pastor of the main church in Casa Amarela was a dedicated monsignor. His parish was huge. He was alone and very much overworked. We helped him out many times when he was ill or had to be away. There would be a dozen or so weddings every Sunday afternoon, each a half-hour apart. I can't remember how many baptisms. Huge crowds at all the Masses. The monsignor died, just before I left, of a massive heart attack while in his early fifties.

Monsignor Osvaldo was the Vicar General of the archdiocese. He came to visit me when I was pastor of St. Boniface in Detroit. After I got married, my wife and I visited him at his parish in Boa Viagem, the "Grosse Pointe" section of Recife.

Perhaps our closest friends were the American priests of the Oblates of Mary Immaculate, OMI priests, for short, who staffed two parishes on the far side of town, one in an extremely poor area, the other in part of Boa Viagem, where people were much better off financially. I'm afraid to try to remember their last names, but there were **Fathers Jim, Darryl (called Dario), Boniface (Bonifacio)**, and several others.

I frequently saw one of the other OMI priests years later when he was in the Milan, Michigan, federal penitentiary. (I was a regular visit for a few years helping Spanish-speaking inmates make the Cursillo and its follow-up.) He had fled the country when Dario was imprisoned by the military. He was imprisoned here for protesting our military buildup and entering a missile site. His dedication is similar to other activists that I admire, like the Fathers Berrigan. These OMI men did wonderful work.

The Dedication of The Monroe IHM Religious

I can't say enough about the wonderful work of the Sisters, Servants of the Immaculate Conception. They not only helped develop our programs, they did great work in empowering the women of the area. The sisters also got involved in helping local Brazilian religious orders update themselves and worked on spiritual retreats for nuns of the area. Later, they helped empower women who worked in the sugar cane fields.

I remember how we officially welcomed the IHM nuns to the parish. **Dom Helder Camara**, our archbishop, came long with his auxiliary bishop, **Dom Jose Lamartine**. We hired a "samba school" of musicians and dancers to lead a procession with almost a thousand people up to street as we came from the airport and entered Nova Descoberta's only street. We had loudspeakers broadcasting the music and speeches for all on the nearby hills to hear! The parishioners made cookies and cakes and gallons of Kool-Aid!!!

The parishioners and the archdiocese of Recife have been enriched by every IHM sister who spent part of their lives in Nova Descoberta! The IHM Sisters maintain a mission in Recife to this day.

Parish Council Votes to Give Electricity to Prostitutes

I don't know if this set a precedent. I do believe that very few Parish Councils in the whole world have made a decision like this.

Let me explain the setting. At that time, it cost the equivalent of twenty-five American dollars to have electricity installed in your home. That included the cost of the meter, Few poor people could ever get that much money together at one time. So, some "entrepreneurs" ("operators") would get neighbors to chip in (often getting more money than needed) on the promise to string wires from the meter to their house. In a poor neighborhood like ours, you had wires going every which way, installed by amateurs, possibly dangerous. These entrepreneurs would tell the home owners how much they owed on the monthly bill, normally bringing in much more each month than was needed to pay the bill. If you didn't pay the bill on time, your "provider" simply cut the wire leading to your house.

It was seven o'clock at night. It was already dark. I was living alone. There was a knock on the door. I turned on the porch light and opened the door to find two beautiful women. They were stylishly dressed, wearing high heels and had nice make-up and hairdos. Not over done, nor over sexy.

They explained that they were sisters (blood sisters) and were prostitutes. They lived in a small home adjacent to the church with their children and their mother. They hadn't paid their electric bills because their mother was ill and they had many medical bills. Their "provider" had cut their wires and their mother and their children were using candles to see by. Could I string wires from the church to their home until they had time to get enough money together?

Wow! What to do? Aha! I had an idea. I had organized a Parish Council and its first meeting was that evening. (So I could put the blame on the Council for any decision!) With my most serious and solemn face I explained that this was a matter for the parish council and they would meet tonight. The women would have the decision tomorrow! I was off the hook.

I never saw such understanding and compassion as with that Parish Council. They discussed it. There was no mention of "What would people think?" There was just a concern for the mother and her grandchildren struggling without lights. They unanimously voted to provide electricity to the prostitutes for three months so they would have time to get money to pay their provider. I was proud of them and slightly ashamed that I didn't have the courage and compassion that they showed that evening. I did get over that though.

It turned out that I would meet these women every so often in front of, or in, the lobby of one of Recife's better hotels. They always said hello. Now I knew why they were there.

Adapting The Cursillo: Fermento

When we wanted to start the Cursillo, I asked the archbishop, Dom Helder, if he would approve it. He was delighted. He said the Jesuits wanted to start it but he had put them off. But if we were going to start it and add a social action component, and especially if the poor were to head it up instead of the wealthy, he would support us in every way!

So I flew down to Sao Paolo and spoke to the Cursillo team there. I arranged to bring seven or eight local men down there from our parish in Recife to make the Cursillo, to learn the process so that they could come back and start it.

When the men were preparing, some told me they would be embarrassed wearing thongs on their feet in Sao Paulo, but they did not own any shoes. I gave them some money to buy clothes and shoes for the trip. Only two bought shoes. One man bought "normal" leather shoes. One other, wanting to save me money, bought molded plastic shoes, which looked like real shoes but had no flexibility to them. His feet really hurt him throughout that whole trip. But he looked good.

In Sao Paolo, the Cursillo participants were still singing "*De Colores*", the retreat's theme song in Spanish. I translated it into Portuguese for us to use in Recife, so it was more Brazilian. It began, "*Das Cores*". Once we returned to Recife, we changed the name of the retreat to "*Fermento*" and started to work with the men to prepare for our first retreat.

Mike and I decided that no one could make our Cursillo unless they had completed the fourteen weeks of discussion using our adaptation of "*The Family of God*" catechetical approach.

The team finished preparing, we selected the first group of 30 or more men, we arranged to use the grounds of the Salesian school on a high hill west of town, we borrowed cots, pillows and blankets and got a couple of trucks to get us there, first with our beds and equipment and then to bring the men.

It started to rain, heavily. People wanted to cancel it. I decided we were going through with it "come hell or high water".

God was sure with us. The retreat came at a time when it was needed. I don't know about hell, but the high water sure came. We got through, even having to cross a raging overfilled river by wading through with the truck.

We finished three days of motivating these men, including urging them to do things for others. When we returned to the parish, we discovered that, after eleven days of continuous rain, the torrential rain was washing

away the sides of many adobe homes in the parish.
When the walls turned to slimy mud, they no longer
support the roofs, which then caved in. Mudslides
washed dozens of houses down the hillsides.

One dad told me he called his son to join him at a
neighbor's home next door. The son obeyed immediately.
If the son had not responded at once, he would have
been washed away down the hill and buried under the
mud and debris of eight or nine homes. Over 4,500
people in our area became homeless within a matter of
days.

The men who had taken part in the Cursillo retreat took
the leadership in rebuilding homes in the area. We were
so proud of them. So was Dom Helder. Many parishes
had similar tragic cases of homes being destroyed. Our
parish was the only one where laymen took the lead
responding heroically. In other parishes, the local priest
was in charge of rebuilding.

The Fourth Choice: Coming Home

In early 1967, I began to feel that I should return to the
States. It was another major decision in my life. I wrote
Archbishop Dearden and he said he would bring me
home in a few months. Meanwhile, **Father Herb
Mansfield** had arrived. He was a wonderful young priest
and who put himself wholeheartedly into work with the
youth of the parish. That was an area we had neglected
in our efforts to concentrate on married couples.

The military was tightening up and beginning to spy on all
of our activities. We had to be careful of what we said
and did.

I left Nova Descoberta in March with a heavy heart. I felt
we had started something but, for me, it was not meant to
last. I knew we had brought an awakening and

empowering to a good number of people in the area. By my count, we had involved over 2,000 adults in our weekly meetings in the homes on the hills, and some 200 men and women in *Fermento*, who would feel the impact of those retreats for the rest of their lives. We had done some good, but I personally needed to move on.

Looking back: How Should Missionaries Act?

When I returned to Detroit, I was sent to help out in Erie, Michigan at St. Joseph's Parish. In June the pastor retired and I was named the administrator. At that time I was considered too young to be a pastor.

Erie was a wonderful place to be in 1967. Migrants came there every year and I already knew many of them who had been coming there for many years. I also already knew many of the farmers.

It gave me time to think about many aspects of missionary work and what advice I would give to priests and nuns contemplating doing work in foreign countries. On the fourth of July, things were particularly quiet so I sat down and typed out my advice to those who would be foreign missionaries.

I chose six topics and elaborated on them from how far to go in adaptation of the culture, in participation in revolutionary activities, in living poorly, in approaches to involve and develop the people with whom you worked, in empowering people, etc.

My brother, Gene, at that time a priest working in Washington, DC, was impressed. He arranged for it to be published in a magazine that had circulation throughout the world. The only other major article in the magazine was written by **Cardinal Suenens**, a famous European bishop. Soon after, Margaret Meade wrote me a letter saying I had given solid advice. A Maryknoll priest working in Peru wrote that his superior had used the article for a full day discussion during a priests' retreat in Peru. When I received these letters, I felt I had made some contribution to missionary thinking; it was worthwhile to have written my thoughts down on paper.

Lucille Cousino and Nancy Jacobs

I liked all the people in Erie, but I loved **Lucille Cousino**, an elderly widow that could banter with me and we could kid back and forth. Lucille helped me out in many ways, but mainly cooking at the rectory fairly often for me and the associate pastor, **Fr. Al Miller**. I also loved **Nancy Jacobs**, a wonderfully gifted girl who has born with some handicaps, principally shortness and a hunched back. She was also born with a great sense of humor. Nancy was the parish secretary. Nancy and Lucille came to Natal, Brazil, after I was married and stayed with us through the wonderful week of *Carnaval!*

Lucille and Nancy helped me with a couple of "pranks" which I will tell you if you promise not to tell anyone.

First, there was a wedding mix-up. I will accept the blame. I knew I had a ten o'clock wedding on Saturday. I knew the family never came to church so I hardly knew them. I also remembered, too late, that the bride's mother had me promise to have a good organist and a professional singer to sing Schubert's *Ave Maria* during the offertory of the Mass.. Of course.

I forgot to tell the organist. So, when I saw the wedding party start to arrive, I made a hurried up phone call to the home of the regular organist, who had left forty-five minutes earlier after playing for the 8 o'clock Mass. The organist's mother informed me that the organist was going shopping in Toledo directly from the earlier Mass. "Do you know who her substitute organist is?" I asked. "I have no idea", said the mother.

Now what? Aha! Father Miller plays the organ. I asked him, politely. He said "No way!" Politely. He didn't feel good enough. But he did agree to celebrate the Mass and the ceremony.

I remembered that Lucille Cousino was taking piano lessons. I called her. It took some fast talking, but I was from a family of eleven kids and had learned early the art of convincing. She said she would do her best but we'd have to start without her.

That was the first and last time I ever played a church organ. The wedding march was played, one long note at a time, somewhat to the tune from the *Song Of Music*, "Doe, a deer, a female deer, ray, a drop of golden sun, me, a name I call myself..." I played slowly and solemnly, keeping my head down so the mother wouldn't know who it was.

Lucille arrived. She played the organ somewhat decently. However, she refused to sing the *Ave Maria*. I sang it while sitting on the floor of the choir loft. Then I ran out and didn't return to the rectory until it was time to hear confessions at three in the afternoon.

You'd Have To Know Paschal

Nancy helped me with Paschal. I was out in the country. The garage for the car was really a barn. There were no nearby neighbors to be bothered if I kept an animal in our garage. As a matter of fact, we had a joke about one priest raising a pig by using it as his garbage pit after each meal. He was really a city boy, the story does, so when it got too fat, he gave the pig away thinking it was wearing out. He got a new little one.

So in November, I bought a little lamb, a bag of oats and bales of hay to feed him and straw for his comfort. I called him Paschal. I planned on eating him on Holy Thursday. Seemed fitting.

The children from our parish school next door loved Paschal. I kept him tied on a long rope in our garage/barn. Every noon, children would come to see him and most would give him part of their lunch. Fruit, peanut butter sandwiches – all kinds. He just chomped them down. He grew larger every day.

Sheep make certain noises that sound something like "Baaa, Baaa." They repeat it over and over. Paschal liked to do it at night. Especially late at night under Father Miller's window.

By March, Father Miller had suffered too much. Earlier he had complained, several times. Now came the ultimatum: "Either Paschal goes or I go", he told me.

I finally decided that I would let Paschal go. I arranged for his beheading and preparation for lamb chops, lamb roasts, etc. I quietly snuck them into our freezer. Father Miller had insisted that I was NEVER to feed Paschal to him. I didn't do it, the nuns, unwittingly, did it.

Nancy was kind enough to bargain with the superior at the convent, **Sr. Margaret Babcock, IHM**. (I got to know Sister Babcock better and can assure you she is a wonderful religious woman!) Nancy told her that the pastor was supplying the meat if they would invite him and Father Miller to enjoy Holy Thursday dinner with them.

At dinner, one of the nuns asked if this was Paschal they were eating. Several looked at me, and stopped to eat as they did. I laughed and said, "You don't think I would do that to you, do you?" They all laughed with me.

I really didn't lie, dear reader. You understand.

What To Do With Left-Over Get Well Cards

Nancy and Lucille both helped me with another prank which lasted for several years. (The reader should note that I have since reformed and changed my ways.)

Father Miller told me his doctor was hospitalizing him for four or five days for a thorough examination. So before he entered the hospital, I purchased five "Get Well" cards and even mailed one to him before I drove him to the hospital. I mailed a card each day. But on Wednesday, he told me he was coming home on Friday, which would leave me with an extra card. So, for the fun of it, I had Nancy sign the extra "Get Well" card with the names "Bev and Bill".

When I picked him up on Friday, he told me he had gotten my card and one from "Bev and Bill". He didn't know who they were and I told him I had no idea who they were.

I added to it. Just before Christmas, I had Nancy sign a Christmas card, again signing with the names Bev and Bill. I even put in a dollar bill, figuring he would know it was real for sure if he got money.

In February, Lucille Cousino told me she was going to Florida for two weeks. Now, I had saved some nice postcards from my last trip to Florida. I had an idea. I had Nancy address one of the postcards to Father Miller and write on it as follows: "I'm here in Florida recuperating from the accident. Bill is still in the hospital in Toledo. Please look in on him. (signed) Bev."

A few days latter I asked Nancy where Father Miller was. I hadn't seen him all day. She told me that he was spending the whole day going from one hospital to another in Toledo looking for a "Bill" who was probably Catholic and from some town around Erie in Michigan.

So I never told Father Miller who was responsible.

I did, however, send him a Christmas card every year for several years afterwards, always signed "Bev and Bill". And, of course, with a dollar bill inside.

Marriage Encounter

Father Jerry Fraser was one of the outstanding young priests of the archdiocese. Jerry was into everything. I admired him, but just couldn't keep up with him. It was Jerry who got me involved with the "Jocist" movement and the *Young Christian Workers*. (The *Jocist* movement was a social-involvement action program originated in France. It included the *Christian Family Movement*, the *Young Christian Workers*, *Catholic Action*, etc.)

Jerry called me one day when I was in Erie to say that he had 10 couples in Detroit who had come over from Spain to start the *Marriage Encounter* movement in Detroit. They only spoke Spanish. He asked if they could put on one of these three day retreats for married couples at our parish in Erie.

Why not? I had plenty of warning. Three days to find Spanish-speaking couples to give up three days this coming weekend, time to get bedding, food, cooks. And, he insisted, the midnight snacks on the last night, Saturday, should be t-bone steaks and whiskey for everyone. Sure.

We had the retreat. Sixteen couples attended this first *Marriage Encounter* in the archdiocese. Jerry soon translated everything into English and the movement had a great start in Detroit. Meanwhile, I felt that it had strengthened and greatly helped the family life of those Spanish-speaking couples in Erie.

Erie Is Not Dreary But They're Shooting Up My Town

I loved Erie and its people. We had a parish mission where we involved hundreds of parishioners and tried to visit every dwelling and inhabitant within the parish boundaries, working in a different area each week for seven weeks during the summer.

The goal was to have everyone meet their neighbor, whether they were Catholic or not. The IHM Mother General allowed nine nuns to stay most of the summer. We tried to have a priest or a nun have coffee each morning with a separate group in the area, and lunch or dinner with a different family.

Theoretically, we could bring the church into 66 homes each week for seven weeks and touch many more lives. Then we had a backyard Mass every Friday in the area, inviting everyone from the area. At the end of the seven weeks we ended with a special Mass in the church.

We didn't touch every single family in the area, but we made a friendly impact. A large number of people now knew one or more of the priests and nuns, and they got to know them in a neighborly way in a friend's home.

I loved the 42 families of **Cousinos** and the 22 **LaPointe** families, but also **Joann and Ted Norts**, the **Paul and Dolores Steinman,** and the **wonderful Latinos** and the dozens of other exceptional people.

We even changed the words to "*Edelweiss*" the song from the *Sound of Music* to have a "parish song" and had special decals made up with a picture of the church on one side, and a prayer to St. Christopher on the inside, with his likeness in a grey-tone behind the words. If they came to have their car blessed during the week of his feast, we inserted one of these decals in the left lower corner of the windshield on the driver's side.

It was fun being there with such nice people.

But that summer of 1967 in Detroit, there was a rebellion among the African-Americans.

I called my mother who lived off East Jefferson near the Belle Isle Bridge and invited her to join me out in the country in Erie. Dear old Mom. I guess, if you raised eleven kids, there isn't much that would faze you either. She calmly replied, "George, don't worry! The shooting's a block away!"

But, as nice as Erie was, I was missing "the action" of what was happening in Detroit. I contacted the archbishop's office and the following June I was transferred to be pastor of St. Boniface Parish, near Tiger Stadium and next to Father Kern at Most Holy Trinity Parish.

The St. Boniface Job

There was a good, socially conscious assistant pastor at St. Boniface who was doing a good job with innovative ideas. His name was **Fr. Norman LeZotte**. I had the impression that he thought he should have been made pastor. I couldn't let that bother me, however, since it wasn't up to him or to me to make appointments and here I was. We got along as best we could, that's all I should say.

St. Boniface had a very mixed congregation of Latinos, Maltese, Native Americans, old Irish families, people from the Appalachian areas of Kentucky and Tennessee, and many African Americans who originally came from the South.

The parish owned seven buildings, a <u>church</u>, the <u>priests' house</u> (rectory), <u>school</u>, <u>janitor's home</u>, the <u>IHM sisters' convent</u>, a <u>separate convent</u> that housed the five sisters from Tlalpan, Mexico who worked with the Spanish-speaking, and a <u>house that was used for meetings </u>and for daily Mass, with the first floor rented out to the City of Detroit.

Besides myself, the rectory housed **Father LeZotte** and his "**assistant**" (a young layman who helped him in social service projects), a **Maltese priest, Fr. Jack Lajoy** who was a hospital chaplain, and normally at least one other visiting priest. This meant that it was necessary to have at the rectory a full time staff which included a parish secretary, a cook, and a housekeeper, as well as a two-day a week laundress. Of course we had to provide for the priests' salaries and the salary of Tom Considine, our saintly maintenance man. An expensive operation.

The school principal was **Sister Josephine Sferrella, IHM,** who did a great job in spite of very limited resources. The school, too, with eight grades and a kindergarten was very costly to the parish, since we could not ask for or receive sufficient tuition to pay all the bills,

St. Boniface parish also had a large part of the responsibility for St. Vincent High School, located but three short blocks away, not just financially, but giving support in many ways.

Our collection averaged about three hundred dollars a week, significantly below the thousand dollars a week that the smaller parish in Erie, Michigan averaged.

In order to pay our bills, we had to borrow over one hundred thousand dollars from the Archdiocese, money that everyone knew could never be repaid. The archdiocese was supporting to a higher or lesser extent some sixty churches in Detroit. Everyone knew this could not continue indefinitely. Something had to be done.

So schools were consolidated, some were closed. Cutbacks were made wherever possible. I took part in planning what was to become *Southwest Detroit Community Mental Health Services* with **Rev. Bill Moldwin**, a local Lutheran pastor. I must confess that I was motivated less in assisting the mentally handicapped than I was for the reality that I could rent them our rectory. Then I could stop paying a cook, laundress and housekeeper, thus saving the parish hundreds of dollars every week!

It worked. I took the $300.00 they paid me in rent, split it with Father LeZotte and we each used the funds to rent our own place in the area. I didn't ask permission to do this, I just did it.

I felt good in my second year there that we were saving the archdiocese money.

Can't Have All Rich People: Sending A People's Representative to Rome

The announcement came out that Detroit's **Archbishop John Dearden** would be made a cardinal, the highest position outside of being pope, that a cleric can reach in the Catholic Church.

I was very happy for him because I felt he was a credit to all of us.

However, I was not happy when I read in the following week's issue of *The Michigan Catholic* the names of the large number of Detroit-area Catholics that would accompany Archbishop Dearden to Rome for the ceremony, along with the various parties and receptions.

The people traveling with the Cardinal-designate were all wealthy, and, as far as I could determine, they were all white. Not one African American, not one Hispanic, and definitely not one ordinary Catholic who was of a lower economic status.

I decided to remedy that. I only had one day to do it, if the person selected was going to be there in time to participate. I asked **Mrs. Hattie Watson,** a wonderful woman who lived on Seventeenth Street, had a family, and a husband who was ill. She worked as a maid in Birmingham, Michigan. She was a solid Catholic and a member of our Parish Council. She was Black and she was poor. Best of all, she agreed to go. Then I called all my friends and relatives to raise the money for her airfare and expenses. That was easy to do but time consuming to run around and collect it. I spoke with the local travel agent who would get her on the plane the next day at noon.

The people at the State Department were wonderful. They agreed to have a passport for her in the lobby of their Chicago office, all they needed was a passport photo and a birth certificate. Unfortunately, she was born at home on a farm in Mississippi and her birth was never recorded. The gracious worker in Chicago told me then that she would accept a letter from any relative of hers who would state that they knew Hattie had been born on that date in that place.

I called the hotel in Rome where the Detroit people were staying because my dear friend, **Lucille Cousino**, from Erie, Michigan was there. Darling Lucille, agreed to take Hattie in her hotel room and make sure Hattie was part of everything.

Hattie and I ran around downtown Detroit all morning (we had to wait for places to open to get passport photos, run to her aunt's house for a letter about her birth, etc.). It was 11:10 when we stopped at her home, so I told her that she had two minutes to say goodbye and to pack for the week's stay. She jammed clothes into her suitcase and away we sped.

Speed we did. A fellow from Skid Row had said he wanted to talk to me. Since I hadn't had time to stop to talk, I had him sit in the back seat. We went very fast, up to ninety-five miles an hour, running along the road-side to pass slower cars when necessary.

We pulled up at the airport and I left the car with the motor running, an unknown frightened man in the back seat, as I ran with Hattie to get her on the plane. All she had to do in Chicago was to take a taxi to downtown, have it wait for her while she got the passport and she should be able to make it back to the airport in time to catch the plane to Rome.

This was one more day when I was very proud of Father LeZotte. He was thoughtful enough to fly to Chicago and make sure everything there went smoothly for Hattie.

When we got back to Detroit, I gave the fellow from Skid Row a dollar. He never did tell me what he had wanted to talk about. He never came back either.

The Vicar And Called A Communist Again, But This Time By Priests

Times were changing rapidly during the 1960's. There were demonstrations held almost every other week against the war in Vietnam. I took part in as many as I could. Kids were getting into drug addiction in large numbers. Many were coming to the rectory with their problems. The Civil Rights Demonstrations were taking place. Many of my priest friends were leaving the active ministry and getting married. It was mind-blowing and beginning to get to me.

I had been called a Communist several times and each time it did not disturb me because I thought those who called me a Communist spoke out of pure ignorance of social justice and even Church teachings.

But the time that really hurt me was when I was called a Communist by my fellow priests.

Let me explain how this came about. I had been elected Vicar of the "Core City Vicariate", a grouping of nineteen parishes centered around Downtown Detroit. My election was engineered by my close friend, Father Norm Thomas, pastor of Sacred Heart Parish on Eliot Street near the Eastern Market.

Activist African-American leaders issued what was known as "*The Black Manifesto*", a document addressing the injustices wrought on Blacks since the days of slavery and calling for justice and retribution. Most of us who worked daily with Blacks understood this as a cry for help and for justice in the spirit of **Martin Luther King Jr.** While the language was strong rhetoric, we accepted it as a legitimate plea and not an intimidating threat.

Jim Sheehan, Norm Thomas and I drafted an inner-city Catholic reply. We asked each one of the nineteen parishes to review what we had prepared. We made many of the changes suggested from different parishes, notably giving strong support of Catholic education, and making many references to the American bishops' 1958 statement on racial discrimination. We then held a special vicariate meeting to formally approve this document. It was approved unanimously by representatives of all 19 parishes. We all felt we had a wonderful and sensible response to the Black Manifesto.

I was asked to make a presentation of our document at an East Side Vicariate meeting of priests. Talk about "hitting the fan", my fellow priests started getting up and shouting at me. I was again called a Communist. I was in a very discouraged state as I made my way back to St. Boniface, alone in my car.

Maintaining My Calling

I was beginning to wonder about my vocation. The archdiocese had sent a priest to be counseled by me because he was thinking of leaving the ministry. He challenged me when I stated that I was true to my celibacy because it was the law of the Church. He said that someone should be true because of love of God, not just because of a law! That made me think.

One of my friends, a nun, came to visit me and informed me that many of her religious friends had heard that I was leaving the priesthood. This surprised me since I had been making every effort to stay in my vocation. It was discouraging to hear that gossip was working against me.

I decided to make a retreat with the Trappist monks at Gethsemane, Kentucky. Jim Sheehan went with me. It helped. One of my resolutions was to get better support from other priests.

To accomplish this, I began a Tuesday morning prayer and breakfast group, which later, under Father Norm Thomas's leadership, included lay persons and religious men working in the city of Detroit. It immediately included a social action concept, calling itself the *Detroit Catholic Pastoral Alliance*. They are very active today and a real credit to the involvement of the Catholic Church in the life of Detroit.

Sr. Lois Burroughs, John Humphrey And A Giant Named Tom Considine

Sr. Lois Burroughs, RSM, started to work with me early in 1969. She shared some of the same goals and concepts of parish ministry that I did. She also spoke some Spanish. Lois' brother was a priest and a classmate of my brother, Gene, who was also a priest. As a child, I had even visited their home in Monroe several times with my brother. I need to mention Lois here because her friendship meant much to me in those days. It still does.

I first saw John Humphrey at a basketball game when he was the coach of the St. Leo High School basketball team. He was yelling at a referee for a "bad call" while they played against "our" team from St. Vincent's High School. It was an impression of a man whose path I did not want to cross.

Subsequent to that night in 1969, I have had frequent contact with him to this very day. He later worked with me at *Shar House* in Detroit, he worked with my wife at schools, and we now see him at Mass each Sunday when we go to St. Leo's Church in Detroit where our friend, **Bishop Tom Gumbleton**, is pastor. John has supported us in many ways, taught us much about the African-American culture (and abuse by society).

John Humphrey has come to our home for Thanksgiving dinner for over fifteen years, always bringing with him his own special peach cobbler, large enough to serve twenty-five persons. It has become a family tradition and even our nieces and nephews ask if he will be there with his peach cobbler! Thank God for people like John.

Tom Considine was the well-known but underappreciated maintenance man at St. Boniface

Parish in Detroit. Knowing Tom made visiting Ireland unnecessary. Tom embodied the very best of Irish-osity. He had a wonderful sense of humor, a deep Catholic faith, and a constant trust in God's workings. He made life happier for me when I was there in the parish.

True Friends: Jim Sheehan, Norm Thomas, Frank Granger, Jim O'Connor

Sheehan, Thomas, Granger, and **O'Connor** were close priest friends of mine.

Jim Sheehan has been mentioned often in this book; Jim later left the active ministry and married **Beverley McDonald**. They still are very involved in working on social issues. He and I play chess regularly and serve with **Tom Reaume** as coordinators of the *Chess Club* at the George Crockett Academy in Detroit. We intend to publish an anthology of articles on issues relating to social justice soon. Jim baptized two of our children; our oldest was born in Brazil and baptized by **Father Larry Dunn**, a wonderful friend who took my place at Holy Trinity Church and later succeeded me at Nova Descoberta in Recife.

Norm Thomas is a wonderful and exceptional priest who has been pastor of Sacred Heart Church for many years. He took one of our school buses for a ride one day when visiting me in Erie, Michigan. He was new to bus driving and just wanted to try it out. It would still be in the ditch he explored with it if someone hadn't pulled him out.

Father Frank Granger was pastor of St, Agnes parish in Detroit and was vicar of his area. We worked together on many projects. He traveled with me and Tom Gumbleton one year and I recall having to save him from an unruly crowd in Lima, Peru. Frank had caught a pickpocket's arm while the man had his hand in his pocket. The man shouted that this American was robbing <u>him</u>. We all laughed heartily as I grabbed Frank out of the crowd and we ran down the street. A wonderful priest! His sudden death a few years later was a shock to all of us.

Jim O'Connor was raised near us in Gesu Parish in Detroit. He became a Maryknoll priest and worked many years in Bolivia. He later left the active ministry and married **Mary Holtz,** a former Maryknoll nun who was living with **Mary Lou Beale**, a teacher at St, Boniface School. We have kept in touch with them all of our married lives and they are godparents of one of our children. They currently operate a grape vineyard near the Napa Valley in California.

The Priesthood

I am nearing the end of this book. God works in mysterious ways, leading us where He will and down paths of great uncertainty. But I trust in Him. Life has been good to me. There is so much that I have learned and so much yet to learn.

I have been helped by learning that my priesthood will always be with me; I cannot attend Mass as a mere lay person. Just assisting at Mass, by my presence I am actually concelebrating with the priest at the altar.
I also remember often that each stage of life means that I simply <u>add</u> to my life experiences. I never deny what I had done or what I am. I am proud of what God has allowed me to do and experience.

Looking back I have been able to observe so much. I have been inspired by the Faith of ordinary people. I have seen the tremendous power of Hope that keeps people going even in the depths of poverty or despair. And, with even the poorest migrants, the Brazilian families imprisoned on hillside slums, or the men on Skid Row, I have witnessed the power of Love in sharing and helping another human being. And, everywhere I went, I saw the

God-given gifts of dedication, patience, humility, long-suffering, and self sacrifice.

The Girl From Bolivia

I first met **Mary Lou Beale** in the driveway between St. Boniface School, the church and the rectory. She was a teacher in our grade school, she spoke excellent Spanish. Like me, she had worked as a missionary in South America, working in Cochabamba, Bolivia. She had grown up in St. Gregory's Parish near my home. We had many mutual friends here and on the missions. She took a job in Kansas City, Missouri and left town. She was there when I decided to leave the ministry. I left on August 15, 1970. I called her from Washington, D.C., not long after, and asked her to marry me.

But that's another story.

So it is in the next book!